"[Palfrey] keeps thrilling us with 'marvelously mature' romance and suspense."

—Emma Rodgers, Black Images Bookstore (Dallas)

Enjoy these
powerful, passionate novels by Evelyn Palfrey

Dangerous Dilemmas

"A refreshing spin on the [romance] genre and . . . well worth reading. . . . Audrey is a real person with real problems who has hopes and dreams just like the rest of us."

—*Booklist*

"One woman's journey to self-fulfillment and a premise that's based on a real issue many women face today shows why Ms. Palfrey's writing is on a quick rise to the top with this intensely alive tale about the challenges of life and love."

—*Rendezvous*

"A mature, intelligent tale to set readers thinking about what they would do if faced with the dilemma the protagonist must deal with."

—*Publishers Weekly*

The Price of Passion

"Deliciously fun . . . a tale of romance, red-hot sex, and mystery . . . that will keep you turning the pages."

—*The Austin Chronicle*

"Every woman should read this."

—*Rendezvous*

"Full of plot twists . . . a thoughtful story about a woman finding the strength to reinvent herself."

—*American-Statesman* (Austin, TX)

OTHER BOOKS BY EVELYN PALFREY

The Price of Passion
Dangerous Dilemmas

Everything in Its Place

Evelyn Palfrey

Scribner Paperback Fiction

Published by Simon & Schuster

New York London Toronto Sydney Singapore

SCRIBNER PAPERBACK FICTION
Simon & Schuster, Inc.
Rockefeller Center
1230 Avenue of the Americas
New York, NY 10020

SCRIBNER PAPERBACK FICTION and design are trademarks of
Macmillan Library Reference USA, Inc., used under license by
Simon & Schuster, the publisher of this work.

Manufactured in the United States of America

ISBN 0-7394-2814-4

Special Thanks

To Emma Rodgers, for your unwavering support.

*To Amy Pierpont, Deirdre Dore, and Jane Chelius,
for seeing this through to the end.*

*To Lois Palfrey, for giving me a love of reading—
and for everything else.*

*To John Palfrey, for giving me a love of travel—
and for everything else.*

To Vanessa, for being the best friend a girl can have.

To Darwin, for all that you did.

Tremendous Thanks

To Tina Allen and Jeannye Polk, still *the* romance queens.

To Dorothy Banks, Elaine Carter, Col. (Ret.) Ferdinand Clervi, Sue Coburn, Peggy Evans, Meredith McKee, Charles Pennie, Beulah Bacon Poole, Kalila Stanley, Florence Vann, Myrna Ward, and Barbara Williams, for your insight.

To Nigel Gusdorf, still my electronic wizard.

To the Beachos. It's been one heck of a ride. The tide has no end.

To all the booksellers who work tirelessly against great odds to bring all of us the pleasure of reading. And to those brave souls who fought the good fight and still couldn't keep their stores open. It was a loss for all of us. And to those who are new, I applaud your courage and wish you much success.

To the book clubs who selected my books for your discussion. I hope you had fun. To those who allowed me the privilege of participating, I hope you had as good a time as I did.

To my fellow writers at BWA, RAWSISTAZ, Mosambas, and my sisters and two brothers at ARWA. I've lurked a lot and you've taught me a lot.

To my readers. Your letters and e-mails responding to the survey in *Dangerous Dilemmas* were most times heart-warming, sometimes hilarious, and always appreciated.

Prologue

LIGHT FROM the half-moon cast shadows through the old oaks all around the park, dark and foreboding. A chilly winter wind blew dried leaves across his path through the parking lot. Marlon didn't like being in this place. A man of his stature shouldn't be seen in a place like this. He had to be careful about his reputation—especially now that everything was going his way. The contracts with the city and the transit authority were nailed down, the architect had delivered the final plans for the new center, and even the recalcitrant ones were not fighting him this time.

But he had no choice. He couldn't be seen with her in the bright light of day, much less let her come to his office. As he scanned the park, he didn't see her now, and a frown of worry crossed his brow.

He pulled the sleek car behind a large oak tree, hoping it wouldn't be visible to the casual eye, and killed the motor. He had turned off the lights and locked the doors when he'd first turned into the park. He pulled the gun from the glove compartment and fingered it. No one knew he had it, and no one needed to know. Many nights he left his office late, often even after the janitor had left. And it wasn't in the best of neighborhoods. The thugs were so bold now, one had even burst into a church and robbed the Wednesday-night Bible Study faithful. And this place wasn't even church. This was the kind of place you could expect to get hijacked. And he didn't intend to give up the car. Not his baby. He slid the gun under his left thigh, where it would be within easy reach.

His eyes swept the park again, looking right, looking left. He saw a couple on the walkway down by the footbridge over the little creek. For a hot second, Marlon thought it might have been her, and that she had brought muscle with her. Then he saw that they were hugging each other and staggering. When they reached the picnic table, the man dropped his pants, leaned back against the table, and pushed the woman to her knees. He held the back of her head in his hands. After a while, he roughly pulled her up and pushed her down over the table. Then he bent over her. How could they carry on this way in a public place? he thought. But then, hadn't he done the same thing?

The sharp rap on the window startled him. He recognized her and unlocked the door. A cold wind blew into the car when she opened the door. As soon as she was seated, he locked it again. Even bundled in the overcoat, she was still small and cute, but it was clear that the life she led was taking some toll. Maybe if things had been different, maybe he could have . . . But not now. Too much was at stake. He'd just have to pray over it.

"Give 'em here," he said, skipping the preliminaries. He held his hand out.

Without a word, she pulled the pictures from her pocket and placed them in his hand. He took the miniature flashlight from the console and trained its bright beam on them. His face hardened. The San Antonio Hilton logo stood out like neon. No question it could be the ruin of him. How could he have been so stupid? Maybe the right thing to do was just to own up to it, take his lumps, and start over somewhere else. But it was too late to start over. And he couldn't walk away from the biggest deal of his life.

"And my mother's locket?" he asked.

"It's safe. Safe with the negatives," she said in a flat voice.

The hard gun under his thigh claimed his attention. Maybe he should just kill her. It would be so easy. Just push her out of the car and shoot her. Her body would be found tomorrow. Just another casualty of the times and the lifestyle. Wouldn't even make the paper. But he knew he couldn't do that. That would be the last straw. Even prayer couldn't save him from that one. Besides, he still wouldn't have the negatives. He'd have to figure a way to get them and to get her off his back.

"What do you want?" he asked gruffly.

"I want them to know it wasn't my fault." Her voice sounded small and childlike.

"I've admitted it wasn't your fault. I take all the blame."

"I want *them* to know."

He shook his head. "That would ruin me."

"You ruined me," she said quietly.

Marlon let that roll around in his head, bumping up against the shame he felt at the truth of it. But it didn't change anything. He'd have to figure a way to chill her out—again.

"Blackmail is against the law. I ought to report you to the police," he said, knowing at the same time that the bluff wouldn't work. He knew she was smarter than that. She'd wised up a lot in the last ten years.

"You won't do that." Her voice was quiet and low and certain.

He let out a slow, resigned sigh. He smoothed his mustache with his thumb and forefinger, thinking.

"I can arrange for you to move to California. You can get a fresh start. You can be whoever you want to be. Of course, I'll put in enough money for you to live fairly comfortably, and I'll see that you have a job waiting. There's nothing to keep you here. That way, neither of us will be ruined."

"You just don't get it, do you?" she said, giving him a hard look.

"Okay, well, how about New York? I have some connections there. Or Atlanta? That's where all the young folk are going." He heard the slightest edge of desperation in his voice and cleared his throat to get rid of it before she heard it too.

He heard the click of the door lock. She opened the door quickly, got out of the car, and walked off. He stabbed the button and the window quietly slid down.

"Come back here!" he hissed.

She didn't even break her stride. Desperation and anger snatched the gun from under his thigh, pointed it at her back, and released the safety. He had her firmly in the crosshairs. Slowly, he let the gun down until it rested in his lap. Was it love that held him back? Or weakness? It wasn't either; he had a better plan.

1

RAY HELD himself still, squeezed between the hard end of the pew and the frumpy sister in a flamboyant hat. She was eyeing him as if he were a thick, juicy steak. The tie was choking him. The thin socks pulled at the hairs on his legs. The hard-soled leather shoes cramped his feet. Not because they were too small, but because he rarely wore them anymore. These days he wore sneakers. He felt out of place. He was only here because it was so important to his mother. Her talk about dying wishes and all had dragged him here. She was only seventy-two—and a spry seventy-two at that.

He'd grown up in this church. Well, not this church. The old church. The old sanctuary with the creaking fans, the offering table his father had built, and the old, dark pews. He couldn't remember exactly how long it had been since he'd been here. Ten years. Maybe twelve. This was his first time since the new minister had come, with his big ideas about community involvement, business development, a bigger building. Mostly a bigger building.

Ray just didn't understand why this Pastor's Anniversary thing was so important to his mother to drag him here. What did it mean, except one more year in which the congregation hadn't voted the pulpit vacant? Maybe that in itself was worth celebrating. Personally, he thought it was just an excuse to take up another collection.

He put a placid look on his face, as though he were really interested in the announcements about the coming week's events. From his years in the army, he had plenty of experience masking his real feelings. He dutifully put a respectable bill in the offering plate, then handed it to the usher standing beside his pew. Glancing at his watch, he thought, if the service was over by one o'clock, he could still get a little fishing in before sundown.

When the purple-robed choir rose and began swaying in unison—lean on one foot, tap with the other, lean, tap—he thought of his mother's misgivings about all the changes in the church, and especially her disgruntled pronouncements about "devil's music." But not even that would make her change her membership to another church. To stop himself from snapping his fingers to the jazzy beat, he consciously opened the program and began reading it. He'd read the program from cover to cover by the time the song ended and the organist segued into a slow medley of old-time hymns.

Then he heard the voice. A voice so low and sultry, he looked up. The choir stood stock-still, all of them posed with their hands clasped together, their lips pursed piously. "I Must Tell Jesus." He followed the voice until he saw her, standing alone at the mike. The light that filtered through the stained glass fell across her face. Her demeanor was one of total reverence. The voice reverberated through him, striking a chord deep inside. Vivid memories of the old church coursed through him—the old preacher's sermons on the scorching heat of Hell and the gold-paved streets of Heaven, the old ladies who were gone on to Glory now.

In the choirstand, Bobbie felt the Spirit enveloping her, overtaking her, filling all the empty spaces. It no longer mattered to her that this was her first solo. It didn't matter that the favored soprano, Doretha, was cutting her a resentful eye. It didn't matter that, for the Pastor's Anniversary, the sanctuary was full to the brim, even the rarely used balcony. Nothing mattered, except the feeling. Not a feeling exactly. A surrender. "I Must Tell Jesus." She couldn't even hear her own voice. Only the feeling. Guiding her, leading her through the high notes, the low notes. It didn't even feel as if she was singing. More like praying. Just telling it all to the One who could relieve her burdens. Telling Him her concern with Monika's approaching adolescence. Telling Him about the trouble at school. Telling Him how Darlene's problem was weighing her down. It was a wonder that she remembered the words to the song. But why not? She'd been singing it all her life.

"Raymond!"

Ray stopped in his tracks at the familiar voice and turned to see his diminutive mother through the throng of folk leaving the sanctuary. She wore her usual crisp white usher uniform with the black lace handkerchief in fanned pleats over her heart.

"I'm so glad you came. Wasn't that a fine sermon? Come on, I want you to meet the minister," she said, pulling him through the vestibule.

"Mama, I've got to—"

"Come on. Help your ol' mama down these stairs now. This won't take but a minute."

Ray knew it was going to take longer than a minute, and that she didn't need any help, but he acquiesced just the same.

Toward the foot of the stairs, he had a view of the entire fellowship hall. The woman was at the table on the far side of the room, dutifully filling little glass cups with pink punch. His mother's voice dragged his attention away to the tall, well-dressed minister.

"Reverend Jackson, this is my son, Raymond. He's retired from the U.S. Army and moved back home," she said, her voice brimming with pride. "He grew up here at Mount Moriah, and he's glad to be back."

"Pleasure to meet you, Raymond," the preacher said in a deep baritone voice. "I'm glad you're going to be a part of our congregation."

"Pleasure to meet you too, Reverend Jackson." Ray knew he was expected to say that he had enjoyed the sermon, and that he looked forward to working in the church, but he wasn't one to lie. He hadn't heard one word of the sermon, and he fully intended this to be his only trip to the church this year. His eye found the woman again and he could still hear her haunting voice. He knew she was a woman of deep feeling, and he wondered how deep.

"Brother Harris," he heard his mother say. "Meet my son, Ray."

The flat tone in her voice caused Ray to pay attention. A stocky man in a one-size-too-small suit had joined them.

"Whazzup?" the man said, raising his chin in greeting and extending his fist for a dap.

Ray knew how to do it, but reserved that for men he cared about or respected. Instead he offered his hand in a formal handshake. He noticed that Reverend Jackson cut the man a quick disapproving glance. "Brother Harris is one of my steadfast Prayer Warriors. My right-hand man."

Ray thought they looked like an unlikely pair. The GQ preacher and the behemoth in the cheap suit who sported a gold tooth that matched his gold earring. Ray just couldn't get used to men wearing earrings. He knew it didn't mean what it used to. Still, there was just something unmanly about it as far as he was concerned.

"Oh, there's Sister Betty. Come on, Ray, I know she'll want to see you. Excuse us, Pastor."

As his mama dragged him around the room, showing him off to the old members, introducing him to the ones who'd joined while he was away, Ray told himself he just wanted to make his mama happy. But he knew better. His real reason for allowing his mother to detain him was to get a closer look at the woman.

"Mama, I'll get you some punch," he said, excusing himself from a conversation about the upcoming Ushers' Banquet. "Can I get you a cup too, Mrs. Long?"

Once he got to the table, he was strangely tongue-tied. He stood at the back of the short line watching her. She moved with an efficient gracefulness, an economy of movement. As she handed him a cup, she looked at him curiously.

"Are you new here?" she asked.

"Yes. I mean, no."

"It has to be one or the other," she said with a smile.

"Not really." It sounded flippant, and he hadn't meant it that way.

He saw the look in her eye that said she thought he was playing a game and that she didn't intend to play.

"I enjoyed your song," he said, making sure that his voice sounded as sincere as he felt.

She looked a little embarrassed. "Thank you."

"I like the old songs."

She nodded with a smile. "Me too. What am I thinking about?" she said, wiping her hands on her apron, then extending one to him. "I'm Barbara Strickland. Most people call me Bobbie."

"Raymond Caldwell." He took her hand in his. "Most people call me Ray."

"Oh, you must be Bessie Caldwell's boy."

"I'm her son," he said with a reproving smile.

"Well, of course. I can see the resemblance. She talks about you all the time."

"Then I'm sure she's told you I won the war single-handedly," he said with a chuckle.

"Seems like she did say something like that."

"Don't pay her any attention. I was just a supply officer."

"I thought you were a general or something like that."

He chuckled again. "Not quite. A lieutenant colonel. I worked my way up. Speaking of Ms. Bragging Bessie, I need another cup of your punch for her."

She reached for another cup, but there were none. "Just a minute. I'll have to go to the kitchen."

As she walked away, he noticed her limp, and the bandage on her foot. He followed her to the kitchen.

"Here, let me," he said, taking the tray of cups from her. "What happened to your foot?"

"Damned drawer. I mean, *darned* drawer. My kitchen drawer. It sticks and I have to jerk on it. Well, this time I guess I jerked too hard. Jerked the darned thing right out and it fell on my foot. Hurt like—heck."

"What's wrong with it?" he asked as he set the tray on the table.

"The drawer? It sticks. Didn't I say it sticks? I don't know. Off the track or something. It's been that way for a while. I can't find anybody to fix it. A guy came out once, but he was more interested in remodeling the entire kitchen. Seems like nobody wants to do a small job."

"I do a little woodworking. I could take a look at it for you when I get a little time. Here's my card."

As she looked at the card, Bobbie thought that he must be about her age, and that he must have gotten a lot of exercise in the army. When he'd handed her his card, she'd noticed that he didn't wear a ring. But she'd learned the hard way that didn't mean anything. Why was she having these kinds of thoughts—and in the church no less? What she needed was a handyman. She tucked the card in her apron pocket and looked up at him.

"Do you have any idea what a small job like that might cost?" she asked.

"It wouldn't have to cost a woman like you very much at all. Just give me a call."

Bobbie drew her chin in and stared at him, a frown forming on her brow. What did he mean by a woman like her? What had he heard about her? She almost expected him to add, "I'll take it out in trade." But he looked sincere, even embarrassed, not lecherous as his come-on had suggested. She wasn't interested in mixing business with pleasure.

Ray could tell from the look on her face that his words had come out all wrong, and he felt the heat of embarrassment on the tops of his ears. "What I meant to say is that I wouldn't overcharge you. I didn't—"

"Who do we have here, Sister Strickland? Don't you want to introduce your friend to me?"

They both turned and looked at the woman who had joined them.

"I'm Jeralyn Jackson. The pastor's wife." She draped the fur coat over her other arm and offered him a perfectly manicured hand, graced by a diamond dinner ring.

"Yes, of course," Bobbie said in a businesslike tone. "This is Raymond Caldwell. Sister Caldwell's boy."

"Son," Ray corrected, extending his hand. "Pleased to meet you, Mrs. Jackson."

"We all just love your mother here. She's a pillar of our church. I don't know what we'd do without her."

Bobbie fought to keep from rolling her eyes. Jeralyn made it sound as though she and Reverend Jackson had built the church themselves and Sister Caldwell was a recent convert. Mrs. Caldwell had probably been a member of Mt. Moriah when Jeralyn was born, Bobbie thought. More than once, she'd actually prayed over the way she felt about Jeralyn. The woman was always bragging about her husband. Always dropping a mention of her affiliation with some social organization or city board. Bobbie knew she shouldn't take it personally. Jeralyn was like that with everybody, but Bobbie felt that her comments about "proper child-rearing" were directed to her because of Darlene. Despite his "proper rearing," the Jacksons' son, Trey, was no saint either. In fact, Bobbie thought him a little odd. In their teenage years, he had had a crush on Darlene and had hung around her house. Jeralyn hadn't said much about him in the last few years.

"If you all will excuse me, I need to make some more punch," Bobbie said.

Ray watched her limp into the kitchen, then was drawn back by Mrs. Jackson's voice.

"Of course you know that your mother can be quite obstinate when she sets her mind to something," Jeralyn chuckled.

"Yes, I've known her a long time." Ray completely understood.

"I hope you'll be joining our flock. There's definitely a place for you here. Pastor Jackson was just saying last night how he needs more men to become involved in his prison ministry. Strong men. Like Brother Harris. You're military, aren't you?"

"I was," Ray said, sneaking a peek toward the kitchen.

"Well, that's perfect. Just the kind of man Pastor Jackson needs. I'll bet you know a lot about discipline and guns and everything."

"A little. Could you excuse me? I need to take my mother this punch before the ice melts."

2

"COME ON, Monee. Hurry up. You can't be late for school," Bobbie called from the foot of the stairwell.

"I can't find my pink socks, Granny."

"You wore them Friday. They're in the dirty-clothes hamper. Wear some others. And hurry, we've got to go." Bobbie shook her head. Lord, that child would lose her arm if it weren't attached, she thought, drumming her finger impatiently on the banister and leaning on the stairwell post. The post gave slightly, reminding her of yet another thing that needed fixing. She didn't know whom to call for something like this. Maybe the janitor at the church would fix it for her. Or maybe Bessie Caldwell's boy. Bobbie caught herself smiling at that thought. She remembered his card and that she'd left it in the apron pocket at church. Maybe she should just call Sister Caldwell and get his number. No. Sister Caldwell might read something into that. But why did she care what Sister Caldwell thought? It really was just for business. Maybe she could run by the church on the way home this evening to retrieve the card. She saw Monee at the top of the stairs in her white jeans, pink T-shirt, and matching socks.

"Monee, you didn't take those socks out of the dirty-clothes hamper, did you?"

"Granny, it's my only pink pair. I had to."

"Monika Tanisha Strickland, if you don't go put on some clean socks—"

"Aw, Granny, please."

Bobbie's brows knitted in stern disapproval. What would it look like for a school principal's granddaughter to wear dirty socks to school? If they weren't running late, if the child had had breakfast, if she didn't have an early meeting with a parent, she would never let Monee get away with that. She would never have let Darlene or Darby get away with it.

"Okay, Monee. Just this once. Just hurry."

Bobbie just had a soft spot for this child. She turned to get her keys as Monee bounced down the stairs, a happy smile on her face and her bookbag slung on her back.

"Careful with that post, Monee. You know it—"

"I know, Granny. I know."

In the car, Monee asked, "Granny, can we stop at McDonald's?"

"Just this one day. The rest of the week, I want you to get up early enough to eat a bowl of cereal."

"Okay, Granny."

Bobbie thought of all the mornings she had gotten up early enough to fix bacon, eggs, and grits, or Cream of Wheat or oatmeal, for her own children. They always went to school with a bottom on their stomach. Of course, as a single parent teaching school, she didn't have McDonald's money back then either. That reminded her that she needed to stop by the ATM on the way to pick Monee up that evening. It was gymnastics night, so there wouldn't be time for her to cook dinner either.

Ray ran the board through the electric planer again, then ran his hand over it. A hint of a satisfied smile came to his face. He clamped the board on his workbench and turned on the router. It bit into the board, cutting the smooth path of the design. He hummed as he worked. He always did. Today it wasn't his usual Temptations song or Jerry Butler. It was "I Must Tell Jesus." That surprised him. *He* didn't have anything to tell Jesus. He tried to change tunes, to substitute one of his favorites, but he couldn't. So he gave in to it. He could see her face, tilted slightly upward, and the serene expression she wore by the end of the song. He understood serenity. It had taken a long time, a lot of sacrifice, but he'd reached that place.

He lifted the router from the board to regain his concentration. He figured he'd be finished with the piece by Friday. Not that the customer was in a hurry for it. And *he* certainly wasn't. When he worked, he was never in a hurry, never on a schedule. He always got a good understanding up front with his customers about that. He'd spent most of his life on someone else's schedule. Now it was only his own. He didn't do this for the money—although he found he could name his price. He loved the wood. Loved the hardness of it. Loved taking a plain board and turning it into a thing of beauty.

Since Sunday, he'd regularly checked the Caller ID thing that his son had put on his phone months ago. He'd thought it unnecessary before, but didn't have the heart to tell Sonny that. Now he could see how it could really come in handy. He thought sure she would have called by now. She had his card. If she wanted him to look at the drawer, she would call. He thought about his gaffe and toyed with the idea of calling and offering an apology. But maybe he should just leave well enough alone. Not call further attention to it. By Wednesday, he knew her number and where she lived. He didn't know why he'd looked it up. It was just that the phone book had been right there. Handy. Sure enough, her name was there. B. L. Strickland on Auburnhill. Thursday night, he sat in his recliner sipping a beer, flipping channels with the remote. Tonight was choir rehearsal night. He doubted even the new preacher could have changed that. He looked at his watch. Maybe he should call and leave a message—just to follow up. Nah. She'd call. He fell asleep in the chair with the TV watching him.

Bobbie was at the stove, stirring in the big pot, and moving her body in time with Aretha belting out "Chain of Fools." When the backup singers sang, "Chain, chain, chain," she held the wooden spoon up like a mike and sang with them. It was Friday night and Monee was at her friend Lauren's birthday sleepover. This was the first night in a long time that Bobbie had had the house all to herself. She had looked forward to it all week. Fresh sheets were already on her king-size bed. Five CDs were in the player, and her plans included a long bubble bath, complete with candles, and her new book—and definitely no alarm clock in the morning. She would wake up on her own around nine, straighten up the house, and take Mrs. Swink a bowl of gumbo. Then she'd pick Monee up. Lauren's mom had been firm about wanting the girls picked up by eleven, and Bobbie understood. Twenty hours with seven squealing little girls would be more than she could bear.

When the doorbell rang, Bobbie looked up from the big pot, wondering who it could be. A frown of irritation crossed her face at the thought that it was probably Darlene. Damn Darlene. Bobbie wasn't sure whom this "tough love" was harder on, her or Darlene, but her mind was made up. If Darlene was hungry, she could have as many bowls of gumbo as she wanted, but not one red cent.

Looking through the peephole, Bobbie could only see shadows cast by the two pin oaks in her yard, and the lone figure of a man in the moonlight. She flicked on the porch light. At first she didn't recognize him. When she did, she drew her chin in and tightened her lips. She opened the door.

"Evening, Ms. Strickland. How're you doing?"

"I'm fine, Trey. And you?" Bobbie made no move to let him in.

"God is good, Mrs. Strickland. All the time."

She wondered if he had learned that at Morehouse College, or wherever he'd been this time. He looked like a replica of his father, down to the expensive suit and polished shoes. Trey had Reverend Jackson's good looks and smooth confidence, but Bobbie had always sensed a strange edge around Trey, even when he'd been a teenager.

"I'm glad you know that. How long have you been back?"

"Not long."

"Have you moved back here, or are you just visiting?"

"I haven't decided just yet."

"Oh." Bobbie thought she knew what that meant. "Did you want something in particular? I'm kind of busy."

"Yes, ma'am. I'm looking for Darlene. Is she here?"

"No, Trey. She doesn't live here."

"Well, I just thought I might catch her here. I saw her earlier today and she said she might come by here tonight."

That explained that nagging little feeling Bobbie had tried to push to the back of her mind all evening.

"Well, I don't expect her. But if I see her, I'll tell her you're looking for her. Should I tell her to call you at your folks' house?"

"Ah, no, ma'am. I'll just check back."

"There's really no need for you to check back here. I don't expect her."

"All right, Ms. Strickland. If you'll just tell her I came by."

"I'll do that, Trey. Good night."

Bobbie closed the door and turned off the porch light. She wasn't a rude person, but she wanted to make sure that Trey got the message. The CD had changed and the sound of Patti LaBelle's voice lifted her spirit. She danced her way back to the kitchen in time with the music. No sooner than she'd lifted the top off the pot, the bell rang again.

Bobbie ignored it, continuing to stir the gumbo. She didn't intend to let Trey or Darlene ruin her good mood. Then the bell rang again. Now, that boy is gonna make me have to cuss him out, Bobbie thought as she marched back to the door. She smoothed her hair and her T-shirt as she passed through the living room. Monee's dolls were scattered about on the couch, and their unfinished Monopoly game was on the coffee table. She'd planned to straighten up tomorrow. With a flick, she turned the porch light back on with one hand and opened the door with the other.

"Trey?" she said to his back.

"Oh, hi," he said, turning back toward the door.

"Oh, I'm sorry," Bobbie said in surprise. "Ray, right?"

"Ray. That's right. Bessie's . . . son." He was surprised that she could possibly be uncertain about who he was. "I was just in the neighborhood and thought if it wasn't a bad time, I could take a quick look at that drawer."

"Well . . ." Bobbie hesitated, thinking about the mess in the living room and the kitchen.

"If another time is better, I can come back. I was just making a delivery nearby and thought . . ." In the face of her inquiring stare, he felt foolish and looked down. "I see your foot is better." He looked back up at her.

Bobbie looked down at her bare feet, then back at him, surprised that he remembered. She could hear her daddy's voice—"Put some shoes on your feet before you answer that door."

"I got tired of fooling with that da—darned bandage. It's okay now."

"Well, it wouldn't take but a minute." Now that he was here and had made a fool of himself, he wasn't going to back down and slink away.

"Well, if you don't mind the mess . . . I was trying out a new recipe." She stepped back from the door, inviting him in. "My friend Wilma makes the most delicious gumbo. She sent me the recipe and I thought that since I have the evening to myself, I'd make a stab at it. Come on, it's this way," she said, walking through the living room and into the kitchen.

"Smells delicious." Looks delicious too, he thought, following her. The red leggings she wore clung to the pleasing curves of her calves. He could only imagine what the long black T-shirt covered.

"I hope it tastes good," she said. "Turns out, the recipe wasn't very specific. A 'pinch' of this and 'just enough' of that. That crazy girl." She laughed. "Or maybe she's being coy. You know, some people won't give you their whole recipe on purpose. Scared yours will be better. And Wilma *knows* I can cook. This is the drawer. Be careful."

Ray tugged on the drawer slightly. He pushed it in and out, concentrating, feeling it. Carefully, he pulled it open.

"Can I take all this stuff out?"

"Here, I'll do it," she said, lifting out the tray of flatware. She gathered up the remaining odds and ends of kitchen gadgets and laid them on the counter, then stepped back. He pushed the drawer back in, then pulled the drawer out until it caught, then pushed it back in. He carefully pulled it all the way out and lifted it off the track. He turned it upside down and examined it, then looked inside the space it had occupied.

"I see just what the problem is. See, this little roller here." He held the drawer up for her to see. "It's worn out."

"So I just need a new roller thing?"

"Yes, and ordinarily it wouldn't be a big problem, but this hardware is no longer made. It'll be hard to find. Maybe can't find it. And see how this piece is glued into the construction of the drawer?"

"Then what?"

"Then I don't know. I might be able to find something to adapt it. Problem is, these kind of cabinets are made of particleboard. They don't hold screws well."

"Oh, well, I should have known. This was a tract house built in the sixties. And not of the highest quality, I might add. Now it seems everything is wearing out."

"Most things do—after a while." He stood the drawer on its end on the floor. He pulled on a couple of the other drawers. "I'm surprised you haven't had trouble with the others."

"I use this one the most."

"If any of the others were the same size, you could just swap them out, but—"

"Say, that's a good idea. Why didn't I think of that?" She reached for the drawer at the other end of the counter.

"Won't fit."

"Sure it will." She pulled the drawer out and turned to him.

Ray stepped out of her way, leaned back against the counter, and folded his arms over his chest. An amused smile crossed his face. Some people just have to learn things the hard way.

"Half an inch too wide," he said.

Bobbie struggled with the drawer but couldn't make it go in. Frustrated, she carried it back to its slot.

"How did you know that?" she asked.

"Trained eye. I'm good down to a sixteenth of an inch."

The sizzle of the gumbo bubbling over drew Bobbie's attention and she rushed over to the stove.

"Have you had dinner?" she asked, turning down the fire and stirring the pot.

"Nope. Is that an invitation?"

"Depends on how brave you are."

"Didn't my mama tell you I won a war single-handedly?"

"Oh, yeah, I forgot," she said, returning his smile. "You have to be a man who takes chances."

"Only calculated risks." He took the spoons and napkins she handed him.

Bobbie served up two stoneware bowls and took them to the table. He waited until she sat, then took the chair opposite her. When she bowed her head for the blessing, he followed suit.

She blew on a spoonful before putting it in her mouth, then watched him expectantly as he took a careful taste.

"Um, this is good," he said, nodding his head. "Just the right amount of filé. Most people overdo it. Or don't put enough."

"Thanks. I'll tell Wilma you said that. So, are you saying I need to get new cabinets?"

"Well, it wouldn't hurt. How long do you plan to be in this house?"

"I don't know. Hadn't thought about it."

"If you plan to be here at least five years, it would be a good investment—especially if you spend much time in the kitchen. And now there are all these organizer things. Bring some order to what you use. Makes everything efficient. A place for everything, and everything in its place. I'll bet you have lots of gadgets that you never use, right? Or worse, you need a gadget, and you know you have it, but you can't find it in all this mess."

"That happens to me all the time," she said with a rueful smile.

"See? You ought to consider it—if you're not thinking about moving."

Moving? He just didn't know. Hard as she'd worked to get this house, the thought of moving had never occurred to her. Well, actually it had, a couple of times this year. There had been a string of burglaries a couple of streets over. But burglary happened all over town, so she had had a security system installed and prayed. Besides, she knew her neighbors. Even though she'd been in the house twenty years, she was the new kid on the block. The house was nearly paid for and she could see light at the end of the tunnel. She was close to her job. Why on earth would she move?

Sure, she had dreams of living in a palatial home, but she never thought she would really have one—unless she won the lottery. She loved the floor plan too. That was why she had bought this particular house. And it had suited her needs and her lifestyle. All the bedrooms were upstairs, and the master was at the head of the stairwell. Through raising Darlene and Darby, that had come in handy. She had always known their comings and goings. The lot was large enough for her to add a downstairs bedroom when the stairs got too much for her—after Monee was grown and gone.

The thought startled her. She hadn't expected she'd be at this place raising a child at nearly fifty, and now that she was here, she didn't want to think about Monee leaving.

"How much would new cabinets cost?"

"Depends. Mostly on the quality of the wood and the hardware. And the craftsmanship. Like anything else, you can spend all the money in the world."

She laughed. "Well, I don't have all the money in the

world. What about if I go to Home Center and just buy some?"

"You could do that. But you wouldn't have much better than you have now. Just newer. They'll look real nice at first." He rose from his chair, took both their empty bowls to the sink, rinsed them, then put them in the dishwasher.

Bobbie watched him with mixed emotions. "Oh, you just taking over my kitchen, huh? You didn't have to do that." She remembered the last man she had had to dinner, a principal at another school. The one who had left the plates on the table as though the maid were gonna get them, slurped up a bottle of wine, then propped his big feet up on her coffee table.

"It's no trouble. Life is easier when everything is put in its place. Come over here. Now look at these cabinets real good. Look at the hardware, the hinges. Come on out to my truck. I'll show you the difference. I'm delivering a bathroom vanity I made for a house under construction."

At his truck parked at the curb, he opened the door to the camper top, let down the tailgate, and carefully pulled the heavy cabinet onto it.

"Run your hand along here. Can you tell the difference?"

"You made this?"

He nodded, a look of subdued pride on his face. "See how these joints are put together? That's called mortise and tenon. They'll never come aloose. Not in this lifetime. You won't find cabinets like these at the Home Center."

"Where are the hinges?"

"Inside. See?" He opened a door and showed her. "Now pull out one of the drawers."

When she did, he could see the look of appreciation on

her face. Ray was accustomed to having the quality of his work recognized, but right now, it was even more important to him that she recognized it. He pushed the cabinet back into the bed of the truck.

"If you're not doing anything, why don't you ride with me to deliver this."

"Oh, I'm not dressed or anything," she said, smoothing the T-shirt.

"You look fine. There's no one there. The house isn't finished yet. It's quite a house too. Worth seeing. It won't take long." He could see the look of uncertainty on her face as she looked back toward her house.

"I don't know, maybe . . ."

"I'd really like the company." He hadn't meant to say that. It sounded as if he were lonesome and pitiful. It was Friday night, and here he was practically begging a woman to go with him to deliver some furniture. It *was* kind of pitiful. And he certainly didn't think of himself as a pitiful guy. But he did want to spend more time with her.

"I guess I could," Bobbie said hesitantly. "I'll have to lock the house and set the alarm. We've had a rash of burglaries in the neighborhood lately. Give me a minute. I need to grab some shoes too."

3

THE INTERIOR of the midnight blue pickup was neat as a pin. Quarters, dimes, and nickels were neatly stacked in the built-in coin holder. A fresh smell emanated from a cardboard pine tree swinging from the rearview mirror. A small notepad and one very sharp pencil lay in the console. Bobbie thought about her own car, with Monee's dolls, scrunchies, and Addy books scattered about.

"So, did you like the army?"

He grunted a wry smile. "I wouldn't say 'like' exactly. I fit in. The army was good to me. I got an education. Got to travel. Steady pay. Good retirement."

"What did you do in the army?"

"I was a supply officer. Bean counter, sort of. Made sure everything was where it needed to be, and on time."

"You didn't build furniture for the army?"

"No. That's what I do for pleasure."

Bobbie tried to think of what she did for pleasure.

Nothing sprang to mind. She was too busy doing things that had to be done. There were several things she had planned to do one of these days just for pleasure—travel, read, teach an adult literacy class. Just when she'd got close to one of these days, Darlene had left Monee with her—and hadn't shown up again for four months. That had been seven years ago.

Bobbie looked out of the truck at the big full moon and wondered if she'd lost her mind. What was she doing on this narrow, winding road with a man she didn't know? Was she really that lonesome? When they rounded a curve in the road, the house came into view. Moonlight reflected off the glass walls of the modern structure. She could feel Ray watching for her reaction, so she suppressed her very impressed *Dayammm.*

Ray stopped the truck in the curved driveway and got out. When he got to her side, Bobbie had already opened her door and was stepping out. At the back of the truck, Ray set the dolly on the ground and dragged the cabinet to the tailgate.

"I'll help you," she offered.

"Nah. I can do it."

"If you can wash my dishes, I can help you with this."

"Well, okay, but you just guide it. Let me bear the weight." His muscles strained at the bulk of the cabinet as he gently lowered it onto the dolly. He set his toolbox on top of the cabinet and wheeled the dolly to the door of the house.

"They let you have a key to this?" she asked as he opened the door.

"Yep. Unless they want to meet me out here every time.

I work on my own schedule." He motioned for her to enter.

Bobbie caught her breath at the grandeur of the two-story foyer and the dramatic ultramodern spiral staircase.

He pushed the dolly into the bathroom. "You wanna give me a hand getting this off?" Bobbie followed him into the huge glass-walled bathroom and pulled the dolly from under the cabinet as he lifted it just enough. He pushed the dolly out of the way and opened his toolbox. "This won't take too long, why don't you look around."

"I believe I will."

When she walked away, Ray set about attaching the cabinet to the wall. He thought that he could have had a house like this if it hadn't been for the divorce. All the years of working, taking orders, making investments, preparing for their future. Then, just when it was all about to happen, only two months before his retirement date, Loretta had him served with divorce papers.

Ray frowned even now thinking about being summoned to the base commander's office to receive them. He'd gone cold all over. At that moment, he was confused and angry. But out of habit, he refused to allow the emotion to show on his face. At first he'd thought it was just some drama play on Loretta's part. They hadn't even had an argument. There had been many over the years. Early on she'd wanted him to get out of the army, had resented the absences when he was away for tours of duty or for training. But when he'd begun rising through the ranks, she'd settled into the role of the consummate officer's wife. She organized socials for the lower-ranked wives, learned to play bridge, and had an uncanny knack for selecting which of the higher-ranked wives to suck up to. All of that had helped boost his career, had brought them closer to his dream of retiring comfortably at a young age, when they could really live. Later that day, he'd suffered the humiliation of packing his clothes while Loretta stood by watching, and an MP was stationed outside their front door.

Initially, he'd made the obligatory tour of the Officers' Club to keep from going to the bare apartment he'd rented, but that hadn't soothed him. So he'd turned to the things that did—his saws and routers and planers. Loretta had had the decency to let him come back for them the day she moved out of the white-columned, two-story house they'd shared during his last tour. It wasn't until he got to court that he realized he would lose half his retirement and half his investment accounts. He wasn't poor by any means, but he sure as hell couldn't afford a house like this one now.

Bobbie walked through every room of the house. The carpets hadn't been installed yet, nor the wallpaper hung, but the structure was beautiful. High ceilings graced every room. The outside walls were mostly glass. She could only imagine living in a house like this. She would spend a lot of time in the kitchen. It was part of the den, with only the counter holding a triple sink to separate it. She imagined herself washing dishes at the sink, watching the moon's reflection on the lake through the windows across the room. Then lounging on a butter-soft leather sofa in front of the massive white stone fireplace. She could forget all her problems in a room like this.

"I'm done. Are you ready?" His voice broke into her reverie.

"Sure." She gave one last look around the room, then followed him to the truck.

Instead of closing the tailgate, he dragged over a small cooler and pulled out two bottles. "Beer?"

"Sure," she said, accepting the bottle from him. She sat on the tailgate with the cooler between them.

"Oh, I could stand this," she said, absorbing the peacefulness and quiet of the night.

"Could you really live way out here? All by yourself?"

"I'd get a big ol' mean-looking dog. Maybe a gun. But, yep, I could love it. What about you?"

"I'd build a workshop right over there." He pointed to a grove of trees just beyond the house. "I'd put a glass wall on the side that faces the lake." He took another sip. "So why didn't I know you, growing up?"

She chuckled. "I guess because you didn't grow up in Houston."

"Houston, huh? What brought you to Austin?"

"College. At first. Huston-Tillotson. Class of '72." A measure of pride sounded in her voice. She didn't add that it would have been class of '70 if it hadn't been for the babies. She'd had a taller mountain to climb than most of her classmates. And driving to Houston every weekend to be as much mama as she could be to her twins had kept her from participating in the social activities on campus. But she'd been determined. Now the whole four years of college seemed like one big blur. All six years, in fact. On graduation, she'd moved back to Houston with her parents and the babies and immediately enrolled in graduate school at U of H. By the time she'd finished her master's degree, one of her HT profs had put her in touch with an alumnus who worked with the Austin school district and she had a job. So back to Austin. This time with her babies. But he didn't need to know all that.

"Nineteen seventy-two, huh? That was the year I started Officer Candidate School. Those were some tough months, but I can't complain. It paid off."

"Was Vietnam the war you won single-handedly?"

He chuckled. "The truth is, I was there. But where I was, it was pretty safe. I was in supply. Mostly paperwork. That was when I first enlisted."

"So you were the one who made sure they had enough bombs?"

"Not bombs. Body bags," he said somberly.

"Oh. I couldn't have done that."

"I did what I had to do. I'll admit, I had planned to get out as soon as my tour was up, but then I figured I didn't have any education, no job waiting, and a second baby on the way. So I stayed and worked my way up through the ranks. Figured I could stay in, get an education and retire with twenty years, and still be a relatively young man."

"Sounds like a plan."

"Well, by then I had two kids in college. So I actually put in twenty-five. And I'm still a relatively young man," he said with a self-deprecating chuckle.

"You're lucky. I wish I could retire." Bobbie sighed, a wry smile on her face. Her life had none of the orderly progression that he'd described, and now her retirement seemed a long way off. She hadn't missed that he had not mentioned a wife. But with two kids, he must have one. It seemed that all the ones who seemed to have some on the ball also had a wife. Bobbie had a hard-and-fast rule against dating married men. She'd rather be alone than play second fiddle or be looking over her shoulder. "We'd better go."

"I'm sorry I kept you so long. I was just enjoying your company." Ray took the empty bottle from her, put both of them in the back of the truck, and pushed the cooler back. Bobbie jumped down from the tailgate and he slammed it shut.

4

SOMEONE WAS on the front porch. Suzie could hear them. After thirty-five years in this house, she knew every sound it made. She lay in the bed, every muscle tense. Listening. She knew they wouldn't be able to get in. Even if they were able to get through the two hooks on the screen, there were still the three locks on the solid wood door—plus the chain. Probably was just Ol' Jimbo, anyway. Drunk again. Missed his own porch by two houses—again. She relaxed a little. Or maybe it was that boy down the block. She'd heard the neighbor say he was on that crack. And he did act kinda crazy sometimes. She thought about the way he had taunted her earlier today when she asked him to stop playing that music so loud. It had disturbed her while she tended her rosebushes. No respectful "Yes, ma'am" like the kids used to. Even when she'd threatened to tell his mother, he'd just laughed. His barrage of curses had driven her into the house. Later, she'd gone out to find her rosebushes trampled and broken. She hoped he'd gotten thorns in his feet, even though she knew it was an un-Christian thought.

He was leaving now. She heard the creak of the fourth board before the porch steps—the sound that always told her when the mail had come.

The bedroom was dark, except for the light from the bright moon that shone through the window by her bed, illuminating the picture of Zeke and Mandy on her dresser. Light or no, it was always the last thing she saw before she closed her eyes at night. She didn't even need light to see their faces. Her sweet man. Her precious baby girl. She'd only had her two years before the wreck that awful day in 1942 that had taken both of them from her and had left her crippled. A crippled leg—and a crippled heart.

A shadow crossed the picture. It wasn't her imagination. Whoever it was now lurked at the window in back of the house. Not Ol' Jimbo. He would be too drunk to unfasten the latch on the gate. That boy. He had been in her backyard before. When he was younger, she'd had to chase him away from her pear tree. No pears this time of year. She reached for her cane, her gnarled fingers feeling along the wall. The window. The shadow was at the window. She hadn't locked it. She poked the cane at it, trying to push the thumb lock now, but it was too late. She heard the window's quiet squeak as it was pushed up.

"Who are you? What do you want?" She reached for her eyeglasses on the bedside table.

"Shut up, old lady." The glasses were knocked out of her reach. "Just lay there nice and quiet, and everything'll be okay."

"Who are you? Get out! Get out of my house!"

She struggled to raise herself, using the cane for leverage.

"Didn't I tell you to lay down?" he hissed. He was at the dresser now, riffling through her drawers. "Where is it, old lady? The envelope."

He grabbed her by the front of her gown and dragged her off the bed. She tried to use the cane to get her balance, but it was useless in the jerking and dragging to the dresser.

"Show me, dammit! Where is it?"

"Leave me alone. Go away," she managed to whisper. Her vocal chords were nearly paralyzed with fear. "I have—"

When he jerked her around to face the dresser, she saw the photo of Zeke and Mandy. If her Zeke were here now, he'd turn this ruffian upside down. His big arms, honed from years of laying railway bed, would protect her. But Zeke wasn't here. Even as she was thrown on the floor, she still clutched the cane. But it didn't keep her from hitting her head on the arm of the chair. The pain in her head was greater than any she'd had from her arthritic joints. Her beautiful lingerie sets were being thrown helter-skelter out of the drawers. The things she'd carefully folded and layered with sachet envelopes, things she was saving for a special occasion that never came. The frilly pink one fell across her face, softly kissing her cheek. She lay still on the floor, hop- ing he would think her dead. She could see the mattress half off the bed. Why would this fool think she would hide her money under a mattress? She might as well leave it out on the coffee table. He would never find her money. This devil wouldn't know where to look. Wouldn't even think to look there. Only one person besides herself knew where.

The crash of her lead-crystal perfume bottles hitting the floor, filling the room with a strong, musty odor, made her cringe. But it was the photo that made her mad. She saw it under the broken glass. The cane. With all the strength she had, she swung the cane. Got him right in the knee. She knew it hurt. She heard grunting and a string of curses and felt the vibration on the floor from his hopping around. Then she heard the phone ringing. It would be Bobbie. It must be ten o'clock. Bobbie always called her at ten o'clock to check on her and to say good night. She always called Bobbie at seven in the morning. That was their system. If she could just get to the phone, Bobbie could help her. She dragged herself toward the nightstand, but just as she reached it, he pulled her back by her leg. With what strength she had, she struck the cane against his head. With an angry jerk, he wrested the cane from her and she saw the knobbed handle coming toward her face. She could only put one arm up to block it. The blows landing against her forearm were brutal. But anything to protect her face. Finally she could take it no more and the cane made its intended mark. She was blinded by the blood that ran into her eyes. It tasted salty when it reached her lips. She wasn't afraid to die. She had done her time on this earth. She had nothing else to live for. She would see her Zeke, and her Mandy. The reunion she had waited for all these years would finally come.

Driving back to town, Ray was reluctant to end the evening. It wasn't that he didn't like the little place he called home. He liked living alone. He didn't ever want to be married again. And he wasn't one to have women staying over, marking their territory. But he had enjoyed Bobbie's company. He pulled over to the shoulder and stopped as an ambulance sped by in the opposite direction. The flashing red lights and urgently screaming sirens brought a frown to his face.

"Somebody's got trouble," he said under his breath, shaking his head. "Say, tomorrow's Saturday. Would you like to go look at some cabinets?"

"Tomorrow?" Bobbie thought about the cost and knew it wouldn't fit in her budget. But what would it hurt just to look? Don't be stupid, she told herself, you can't afford cabinets and he's married.

"Mrs. Caldwell might not appreciate that."

"What's my mama got to do with your cabinets?" he asked with raised eyebrows.

"Your wife, silly."

"You mean my ex-wife?"

Now, that's a little better, Bobbie thought. Shopping for cabinets with him was feeling like a fine idea. Then she remembered Monee's piano lesson. "I have an appointment tomorrow."

Ray was glad it was dark so she wouldn't see the look of disappointment on his face. "The whole day? It would only take an hour or so."

"Well, maybe around three o'clock."

"That would be good. I'll come by then," he said, turning on her street.

The flashing lights of three police cars were visible from the end of the street.

5

"OH, MY GOD!" Bobbie's hand flew to her mouth at the sight of the police cars parked directly in front of Mrs. Swink's house. The crowd of neighbors gathered on the sidewalk was eerily illuminated in the revolving blue lights and flashing white strobe lights atop the police cars.

"Pull down there," she ordered. "Jesus, I was supposed to call her at ten. What time is it?" She looked at her watch. "Jesus! How could I have forgotten! I'm supposed to be taking care of her." She hopped out of the truck and reached Jimbo first. When Bobbie grabbed his arm and turned him around to face her, she smelled the stench of old alcohol that usually hung about him.

"What happened, Jimbo? What happened?"

"I don't know. They just took ol' Ms. Swink in the amalam'. Somebody say she got beat up real bad. I don't know nuthin' 'bout it. Don't want no trouble with them polices."

"Why would they give you trouble?"

"Maybe Idalia knows sumphin' 'bout it. She up there talking to that police," he said, pointing. "You know how she just got to know everything."

Bobbie pushed her way through the crowd to where Idalia was.

"Idalia, what's going on? Where's Mrs. Swink? What happened? Jimbo said—"

"I don't know. I'm trying to find out, but this law here won't tell me nothing." She turned to the officer. "Say, I axed you a question."

"Stand back, miss. That's the last time I'm gonna tell you. All of y'all, move on back!"

Bobbie couldn't wait. A trill of panic was rising in her. "Officer, I need to—"

"Back, lady! I said move back!" He gave her a little shove.

"But I—"

Ray's calm voice from behind Bobbie pulled her back from the wild place she was heading.

"Officer, this lady's not trying to give you any trouble. She's the next of kin. She just needs to know where they've taken her, uh, aunt."

"Brackenridge Hospital. Stay right here. The sergeant'll want to ask you some questions. Okay now, the rest of you people, move on back," the officer shouted, walking down the line and motioning the crowd away with his baton.

Bobbie felt Ray take her hand and pull her slowly backward. When they got to the edge of the crowd, he said, "Come on. Let's go."

He backed the truck up the street three driveways before turning it around. All the way to the hospital, Bobbie's lips were drawn tight into a grim line, even when she spoke. "This is all my fault. I should have been home. I should have called."

"This can't be your fault."

Bobbie thought of how many days it had been since she'd been by to see Mrs. Swink. Between her job and all of Monee's activities, she was just too tired. She'd kept putting it off until tomorrow. Tomorrow hadn't come for a week now. But she couldn't just pop in and out anymore. Mrs. Swink always wanted her to stay. To have a cup of tea. To read her an article from the paper now that her failing eyesight could only read the headlines. To help her find some "important paper." Lately, it seemed Mrs. Swink's mind had been wandering around a bit. It took more time for her to complete a single thought. Bobbie hadn't found the time. Hadn't made the time. She had planned to go by tomorrow after Monee's piano lesson. But she'd also planned to go cabinet shopping.

Friday night in the city hospital emergency room looked like a war zone. Mostly wounded women, their children, and assorted relatives. Bobbie found her way to the desk.

"Swink?" the harried nurse repeated. "Yep. She's in seven. But you can't go in. Are you the responsible party?"

Bobbie hesitated. She didn't know what else it would mean, but she knew that a yes answer would get her more information than a no would.

"Yes. What happened? How is she? "

"I can't say." The nurse handed her a clipboard. "The doctor will speak with you in time. I need you to fill this out."

Ray pulled Bobbie away to a seat on the far side of the waiting room. She sat down and stared at the clipboard. Her hand shook so much she couldn't even fill in the blank for "Last name." Ray sat beside her and took the clipboard from her.

"I got Swink. What's her first name?"

"Suzie."

"Auburnhill Street. What's the number?"

"Seventy-five oh five."

"You know her social security number?"

Bobbie fished in her purse for her pocket organizer. She found the number there, along with the listing of Mrs. Swink's prescription numbers. She always picked them up for her when she went to get her own monthly estrogen supply. She knew enough of Mrs. Swink's medical history for him to fill out that portion of the form. When all the blanks that she knew had been filled in, Ray handed her the form to sign. She hesitated a moment, then read the fine print. She sure as hell didn't have the money to pay a hospital bill, but what choice did she have but to sign it?

"Stay here," he said, his hand pressing on her shoulder. "I'll take this back to the nurse and see what I can find out."

"No, I need to know."

They approached the nurses' station together. Bobbie handed the clipboard back.

"I need to know what's going on with my, ah, aunt."

"The doctor will come talk to you soon."

"I've been here long enough for him to come. Surely you can tell me something."

"I'm sorry, ma'am. I'm not allowed—"

"Then get the doctor here now," Bobbie said in as stern a voice as she could muster.

A worried look crossed the nurse's face. "They don't like for us—"

"I don't give a hoot what they like or don't like. I need to know something. And now. What's the doctor's name?"

"I've already called the doctor, ma'am. But he's in surgery now."

"Can't you tell me anything? Just in the name of human kindness and decency?"

The nurse looked down at the papers on her desk, then back at Bobbie. "I'd call her other relatives, if I were you."

Bobbie's shoulders slumped. All the fight was gone from her. Ray put his arm around her shoulder and held her steady.

"That doesn't sound good, Bobbie. Sounds like they don't expect her to live through the night." He looked at the nurse inquiringly. She nodded.

"The police said someone broke in her house," Ray said to the nurse. "I guess they beat her up real bad, huh?"

The nurse nodded again.

"She probably has a head injury."

The nurse nodded.

"And maybe some broken bones?"

The nurse consulted the chart and nodded again.

"And they'll probably operate on her?"

The nurse shook her head.

Ray nodded his appreciation to the nurse. "Come on, Bobbie. Let's go sit down and figure out who you need to call." Ray led Bobbie back to a chair. "This sounds bad. Head injury's the worst. Not much they can do with that. How old is she?"

"Eighty-four, I think."

"Umph. That's why they won't attempt surgery. I think you'd better contact her family. Maybe they can get here before . . ." He gave a slight shrug to finish the sentence.

"She has a cousin. A distant cousin somewhere in Mississippi, but I don't know how to reach her." Bobbie couldn't bear the thought of Mrs. Swink being alone, so she waited for the attendants to leave cubicle seven. She stood and eased to that side of the waiting room. Then, just as though she were entitled, she stepped through the folds of the curtain.

She put her hand over her mouth. That was all she could do not to cry out loud. The body lying on the gurney didn't look like Mrs. Swink at all. Her head was swollen almost beyond human, just a big blotch of red and blue. At least the parts she could see. Most of it was covered by gauzy bandaging. A tube ran inside her mouth and was taped at the corner. Big purple bruises covered her spindly arms. They were frail enough to be hers, Bobbie thought. IV needles were taped to both hands with lines running to drip bottles hanging above the bed. Tears sprang to Bobbie's eyes and ran down her face. What kind of monster could do something like this to poor little Mrs. Swink? Bobbie reached out to touch her hand. She wanted her to know that someone who cared was here. She believed the will to live was more important than all the devices and medicines that the doctors had. She leaned over close to her ear.

"Mrs. Swink? This is Bobbie. I'm here. Can you talk?" There was silence and no movement.

"Who did this to you, Mrs. Swink? Can you tell me what happened?" Bobbie sighed and wiped her eyes.

"It's my fault. I'm so sorry. If I had been home, this never would have happened."

Bobbie saw movement out of the corner of her eye. Or did she? The little finger? Did it move? Bobbie put her hand over Mrs. Swink's.

"You're going to weather this. You've got to. I ain't got time to fool with those rosebushes." Bobbie's choked laugh turned into a cry. "I'll be here. Right outside. As soon as you feel like talking, they'll let me know. I'll come right back. Now don't you worry about a thing except getting better." When she patted the dry wrinkled hand, she noticed that Mrs. Swink's ruby ring was missing.

Bobbie went back and sat next to Ray. For a while neither of them said anything.

"Why don't you leave your phone number at the desk. I'll take you home. Nothing you can do here."

Bobbie shook her head. "I'll stay. You go on. Thanks for everything."

Ray twisted his mouth to the side. This wasn't how he'd imagined the evening ending. But he couldn't leave her here alone.

"I'll stay for a while."

Every time the curtain across the cubicle opened, Bobbie looked up expectantly. Every now and then, Ray checked with the nurse and returned shaking his head. No change. Hours passed. The pace in the emergency room picked up as the night wore on. The opening of the automatic doors to admit another gurney increased in frequency. Another victim. More policemen. More blood. Bobbie pushed her shoes off, tucked her feet under herself, and leaned against Ray's shoulder. After a while, Ray pulled her head into his lap.

In the wee hours, things had quieted some. Bobbie woke, sat up, and rubbed her hands over her face. She spotted the doctor catching a breather by the coffee machine. She walked straight up to him.

"Can you tell me anything about Mrs. Swink?"

"Swink? Swink?" He scratched at his head, struggling to remember.

"Number seven."

"Oh, seven. Yeah. No change."

"That's good, isn't it?"

He looked at her strangely, then nodded. "I guess that's right. That's a positive way to look at it. I'm surprised that she's survived this long. But I don't want to give you any false hope. Any minute, things can change. All you can do is pray."

"I can do that." She turned to walk away.

"But, ma'am?" he called her back. "I don't know what you should pray for. Even if she comes out of the coma, she won't be the same. Her quality of life will be . . . diminished. It would be a miracle—"

"Miracles happen, Doctor."

The skepticism on his face told her he wasn't old enough yet to know that. So much book learning.

Ray looked at his watch. "Bobbie, I hate to do this, but I need to go. It's ten o'clock. I have an appointment at noon."

"Ten! I have to go too. I have to pick up Monee."

"Monee? Who's Monee?"

Bobbie frowned in confusion. Then she realized she hadn't said anything to him about Monee.

"Monee's my grandbaby. She's at a sleepover. But the mother wanted all the girls to be picked up by eleven. And just look at me. I can't go there like this. I need to go home first." She looked at her watch and glanced back toward cubicle seven. "Maybe if I hurry. Let me talk to the nurse."

As she started away, two white-uniformed orderlies approached cubicle seven. Bobbie caught one of them by the arm.

"What's happening?"

"We're moving this one to ICU. A bed finally came available. Nothing more they can do here."

"Can I go with her? I'm her niece."

The man nodded his assent, just as Ray reached her side.

"What about Monee?" he asked.

Bobbie put her hand to her forehead and squeezed her temples, then let out an exasperated sigh.

"Would it help if I picked her up for you? I don't mind doing that."

She hesitated, then looked in his eyes. Should she trust him to do that? What would Monee think?

"I can whip by the house and shower and still pick her up by eleven," Ray said. "But I'll have to take her to my appointment. It's kind of far out on the other side of town, but it shouldn't last too long. Then I'll bring her here. Is that okay?"

Bobbie's thoughts were suddenly interrupted by the sound of an intermittent and urgent alarm. The doctor and two uniformed women rushed into cubicle seven.

"I don't know. She doesn't know you. Maybe . . ." Bobbie saw frantic movement inside the curtain. She made up her mind in a snap. "Yeah, okay. The address is eighty-four oh five Shadow Bend. Just bring her here. Tell her 'blue tree.'" She started toward the cubicle, then turned back and called out, "Be sure and say 'blue tree.'"

6

MONEE STARED at the man, looking him up and down. She didn't want to go with him, but he *had* said "blue tree." So he must be okay. Granny told her never to go with a stranger unless they could tell her their secret code. Granny had let her make it up. Monee thought no one in the world would just think up *blue tree* except her. Still, she would rather not go with him. But Mrs. Lindsey said Lauren had to go to her dance lessons, and Mrs. Lindsey seemed in a hurry to leave. The man seemed in a hurry to leave too. Grown-ups were always in a hurry.

"Can I take your bag for you?" the man asked.

"Uh-uh. It's not heavy."

She followed him to the truck, slung her backpack into the seat between them, and climbed up on the seat. He smelled like soap. None of the men her mother hung out with smelled like soap. Her granny didn't hang out with men.

"Where's Granny?" Monee demanded when he started the truck.

"She had some business to see about. She asked me to pick you up. I'm going to take you where she is. But first I have to meet with a man about some work I'm doing for him. I hope you won't mind going with me."

Monee watched him out of the corner of her eye.

"Why can't you take me to where Granny is now?"

"It just wouldn't work that way. If I did that, I would be late for my appointment. Then the man might think that if I would be careless about our appointment, I would be careless about my work. Do you understand?"

Monee didn't, but she nodded anyway. Grown-ups were always saying a bunch of words to keep from giving her the answer she wanted. She looked out the window. This was a part of town she hadn't seen before.

"Are we still in Austin?" she asked.

"Yep. On the outskirts."

Monee wanted to ask him what an outskirts was, but decided she'd wait and ask Granny. She picked up the pencil and looked at it.

"This pencil sure is sharp," she said, turning it over in her hand.

"It writes best that way."

"How did you get it that sharp?"

"With my knife."

"You have a knife?"

He pulled it out of his pocket and showed it to her.

"It's pretty," she said, taking it out of his hand and turning it around.

"The handle is made of ivory. Don't open it. It's very sharp. I got that when I was in Germany."

"You been to Germany? That's a long way from here, isn't it?"

"You bet," he answered, chuckling. "I was in the army for twenty-five years."

"I'll bet you've been to a bunch of places."

"Yep." He pulled the truck into a driveway and stopped. "You stay in the truck. I'll be right over there. I won't be long. Then I'll take you to your granny."

As soon as he got out of the truck, Monee opened the knife. She reached in her backpack and fished around for her pencil.

When Ray came back to the truck, a frown crossed his face at the shavings all over the seat. The knife lay in the console. The butchered pencil lay in her lap. Monee wore a guilty look.

"I told you not to open my knife. Are you always disobedient?"

When he saw tears well up in her eyes, he got out of the truck and walked around to her door.

"Get out." He helped her down, then brushed the shavings out of the seat.

"You're mad, aren't you?" she asked.

"No."

"Yes, you are. I'm sorry."

"Okay, I'm mad."

"I just wanted my pencil to be sharp like yours."

"You could have just asked me. I would have sharpened it for you."

"Will you show me how to do it?"

"No." Then Ray relaxed his lips and reached in the truck for the knife. He took the pencil from her hand and began shaving it to a fine point. "Don't you try to do this. It takes a lot of practice." When it was just as sharp as it could be, he handed it to her. "Now let's go."

A grin broke out on Monee's face and she got back in the truck. By the time he got in, she had taken his pad from the console and was making letters on it.

"You're not going to tell Granny I've been bad, are you?"

"You haven't been bad. You've been disobedient. What if you had cut yourself? Your granny would have whipped me."

"Why would she whip you for something I did?"

"Because I was responsible for you. She trusted me."

"Granny wouldn't whip you. She just fusses and makes you go to your room."

Ray had to stifle a chuckle as he pulled into the parking lot at the hospital.

Monee's eyes got big. "Is Granny in the hospital?"

"No. She's visiting someone."

When Ray helped her down from the truck, Monee looked up at him.

"Please don't tell Granny I've been bad—I mean, disobedient."

"I don't know . . ."

"I promise, I won't do it again. Can't you just keep a secret?"

"I don't think a grown man should keep secrets with a little girl."

"I have a secret with my mama's boyfriend."

"Your mother's boyfriend? How old is he?"

"I don't know. Antonio's real old. About twenty-something."

Ray wasn't sure he wanted to know, but he asked anyway. "What is the secret you have with him?"

"I can't tell *you*. It's a secret. A cross-my-heart, hope-to-die secret."

They had all been quiet on the ride from the hospital. Ray pulled the truck up to the curb in front of Bobbie's house. He got out and opened the door for them. This time Bobbie waited for him. Ray wanted to mention to Bobbie about Monee's secret, but Monee was holding on to Bobbie's arm and watching him. Bobbie looked as if she'd been run through a wringer.

"Thanks for everything, Ray. I'm sorry you got caught up in all this. And I appreciate what you did."

"No problem. I don't suppose you'd want to go look at those cabinets?"

"Not today. I've got to change and get Monee to her piano lesson," Bobbie said, looking at her watch. "Then I'll go back to the hospital. Maybe another time."

"Can I call you?"

"Sure," she said, unlocking her door. "Monee, hurry and get ready to go to your lesson."

"If you'd give me that drawer, I'll see if there's anything I can do with it."

"Well, I'd hate to trouble you."

"No trouble a-tall."

He left with the drawer.

That night, Bobbie pulled her car into her driveway without daring to look toward Mrs. Swink's house. She'd been so tired she'd slept through Monee's piano lesson. Then they'd gone back to the hospital. Mrs. Swink's condition was unchanged. Mrs. Swink didn't seem to know they were there, so finally at nine Bobbie had come home. She was anticipating a long soak in the tub.

"Mommee!" Monee hopped out of the car and ran up on the porch.

At the sight of Darlene sitting on her swing, Bobbie wearily pulled her purse on her shoulder and got out of the car. Just what she needed.

"How're you doing, Darlene?" she asked, stepping on the porch. She couldn't identify the emotion she felt watching Monee with her arms wrapped around Darlene's waist.

"Hi, Mama," Darlene said.

"What brings you to the neighborhood?"

"I need to talk to you, Mama."

"Not tonight, Darlene. I'm tired. I've been at the hospital with Mrs. Swink since last night."

"What's wrong with Mrs. Swink?"

"Somebody broke in her house and beat her up real bad. She may not make it."

"Oh, damn. Who would do something like that? She's a sweet old lady."

"Yes, she is. And I'm a tired old lady."

"Can you sit down just a minute? I really need to talk to you, Mama."

"About what, Darlene?"

Darlene put her hands on either side of Monee's face and kissed her cheek. "Honey, why don't you run upstairs and take your bath while I talk with Granny. When you finish, I'll come tuck you in bed."

Monee ran into the house with a big grin on her face. Bobbie sat on the swing.

"What is it, Darlene? I'm not giving you any money," she said tiredly.

Darlene took a hesitant step, then sat on the swing next to Bobbie.

Bobbie couldn't stand to look at Darlene's hair. Hair that she had lovingly washed and pressed and curled for so many years until Darlene had cut it off. Now it looked like a rat's nest. And she smelled bad too.

Darlene nervously pulled at her dress. "It's about Monee."

Bobbie jerked around. "What about Monee?"

"Well, uh, I was thinking it's about time for her to come live with me."

"Live with you where? On the streets?"

"I got a place."

"Yeah? Where?"

"It's in a shelter for abused women. I got a room. It's pretty nice."

"And you think I'm going to let Monee live in a shelter for abused women? Why on earth would I do that when she has her own nice, clean, safe room right here? And how did you get a room there? You ain't abused, Darlene. You're abusing everybody else."

"I'm getting myself together, Mama. Honest."

"Well, I'm glad to hear that, Darlene. But you can't have Monee. That child has enough to deal with, without being dragged through your bullshit—again."

"She's *my* child, Mama."

"She's *been* your child, Darlene. That hasn't kept you from leaving her on me."

"I know. I know, Mama. I'm trying to make it right. I got a room now. And I have a lead on a job. And I need Monee with me."

"You *need* Monee? What's this really about?"

Darlene hesitated. "They trying to revoke my probation. But the judge said she would consider letting me stay out since I have a kid. She said if I get a place and a job—"

"So Monee's just a prop in your—"

"That judge is gonna send me to prison if I don't—"

"Prison?"

"You don't want me to go to prison, do you, Mama?"

"Of course I don't want you to go to prison, Darlene. You're my child."

"And Monee's *my* child. If you just let her come stay with me awhile, I think it'll help me too. Not just to stay out of prison, but because I'll have to be a better person."

"How 'bout you try being a better person first for a while? Then we'll talk about Monee staying with you."

Darlene twisted the thin fabric of her dress around her fingers. Her mouth worked in a nervous way as she gathered up her courage.

"My lawyer say you can't keep me from taking her."

"Is that right?"

"Yeah. My lawyer say he can make you give her to me.

He say that grandparents ain't got no rights. He say the court here will make you give her to me, since I'm her mama. In fact, he say I can just take Monee and ain't nothing you can do about it. But I don't want to do that, Mama."

"Well, you just tell your lawyer he can kiss my black ass. It's time for you to go, Darlene. I'm tired." Bobbie stood up.

"I'ma go, but I'll be back. Here's the card from my social worker at the shelter. You can check that out if you want to. There's other kids there."

"Well, Monee isn't going to be there. You can bet on that."

Bobbie stepped in the house, closed the door, and turned the bolt lock. She leaned back against the door and closed her eyes. When she opened them, Monee was standing at the top of the stairs.

"Where's Mommie, Granny? She said she was gonna come tuck me in."

Bobbie let out a heavy sigh. "She had somewhere to go. You go on to bed. I'll be up in a minute."

Bobbie couldn't stand the look of disappointment on Monee's face. "She'll come another time. You want to sleep with me tonight?"

Monee looked down at her foot and brushed it back and forth on the carpet. "That's all right, Granny. I'm a big girl. I'll be okay."

7

IT WAS Sunday morning, and the pieces to the drawer were spread out on his worktable. Ray methodically searched through all the little drawers of screws, nails, and miscellaneous parts looking for just the right piece. He'd started out wanting to fix this drawer for Bobbie, but now it was a challenge for him. His first mind told him that the cheap drawer wasn't worth fixing, but at the same time, he was confident he could do it.

Ray loved the orderliness of his workshop. Peg-Board covered an entire wall, and every tool hung on a prong fitted especially for it. In his tall tool chest, each drawer held like items—one for tubes of glue, another for various kinds of tapes, another for his tiny screwdrivers. The deep drawers at the bottom held his automotive gauges and other bulky tools. He had a place for everything, and everything was in its place.

He couldn't understand why he'd found himself in

church that morning, instead of at the lake fishing as he'd planned. His mama had grinned like a Chessy cat when she saw him there, and he didn't have the heart to tell her the real reason—and he sure wasn't going to explain his disappointment that Bobbie wasn't there. He knew he should be able to just blow her off. The one thing he'd learned since the divorce was that a black man with benefits was in great demand. He could just about have his pick of the women he ran into. But he didn't want just any woman. As his mind wandered to thoughts of Bobbie, his fingers searched the drawers of the tool chest; he just knew he had a little roller somewhere that would do the trick.

Sunday night, Bobbie sat across from Monee at the kitchen table, watching her eat a hamburger while just picking at her own. They had missed church that morning because they had spent the day at the hospital. The doctor's request to take Mrs. Swink off life support had frightened and depressed Bobbie. She didn't feel she was in a position to make that kind of decision. She wasn't really next of kin. More like next of friend. But if she'd told the doctor that, no telling how he would have reacted. He would probably have revoked her visiting privileges. She just knew it was important that Mrs. Swink know she was there. And somehow, Bobbie felt she knew. But making that kind of decision was too heavy a burden for her. It would be like killing a piece of her own life.

Through the years, Mrs. Swink had been more than a friend to her. When the kids were young, Bobbie had never worried about having a sitter. Darby and Darlene went to Mrs. Swink's house after school. And the few times Bobbie had had a date or gone out with her girlfriends or had a late meeting at school, Mrs. Swink had always been available. Bobbie didn't have to worry whether the kids would have a hot dinner or be put to bed on time. Even when Bobbie could afford to pay her a little something, Mrs. Swink had never accepted a penny. She'd always had a special affection for Darlene. Even through all of Darlene's tribulations, even when Bobbie herself had lost the faith, Mrs. Swink always maintained hers. "She's a good girl, Bobbie. She's gonna find herself. Just give her some time." And even though she was now old and suffered with aching joints, she had always had time for Monee. So how on earth could Bobbie tell the doctor to just kill her?

"Granny, is Mrs. Swink going to die?"

"Well, honey, we're all going to die one day. Only the Lord decides when." Bobbie could tell by the look on Monee's face that she wasn't satisfied with the answer. Bobbie decided to tell the truth. "She might, honey. I hope she doesn't. She is hurt pretty bad."

"Is that why you wouldn't let me go in the room to see her?"

"I, well, I just didn't think she'd want you to see her until she's better."

"She wanted to see me, Granny. I know she did. I'm her sweet little Monee. She always wants to see me. Will she be better tomorrow? Maybe I can see her then. I want to take her the Mandy doll she gave me, so she won't be all alone."

"You have school tomorrow, Monee. In fact, it's time for you to get ready for bed."

Monee got up and started out of the room.

"Monee, come back here."

Monee came back and, under the stern look Bobbie gave her, rolled up the ketchup, salt, and pepper packages in the paper her burger had come in. She took it and the drink cup to the trash can. She stopped by the door and turned to Bobbie.

"Granny, is Mr. Caldwell your boyfriend?"

"Of course not. Why would you ask that, Monee?"

"I don't want you to have a boyfriend, Granny. Boyfriends are bad. I just want you to have me."

"Come here, little girl." Bobbie grabbed Monee in a bear hug, then held her out at arm's length. "Granny loves you. And you're all I need. Now you go take your bath and quit worrying about grown folks' business." Bobbie swatted Monee on the behind and watched her walk away.

Bobbie picked up a french fry and put it in her mouth, wondering what Monee meant. The thought of Ray as a boyfriend didn't seem bad to her at all. She gathered up what was left of her own meal and put it in the trash can.

There on the counter lay the card Darlene had given her: "Penelope Dawson, Caseworker, House of Hope." Bobbie picked the card up to see the address and sucked her teeth. Not the best area of town, she thought. Maybe she should call the woman in the morning. Maybe Darlene was really getting herself together this time. Bobbie sucked her teeth again. She'd been around this circle too many times before to get her hopes up. Still, maybe she should call the woman—just to set the record straight. She put the card in her purse. No telling what kind of lies Darlene had told the woman. Well, Ms. Dawson needed to know that come hell or high water, Monee was not going to be her tenant.

★   ★   ★

Bobbie hated Mondays. Even when she'd been in the class-room, she'd hated Mondays. Now that she was the princi-pal, she felt the same way. It was always like starting the school year all over. Thursday was her favorite day. The kids were settled back into the routine and more focused than they would be on Friday, when their little minds were on getting out of school for the weekend. And choir rehearsal was Thursday night and that always buoyed her spirits. But this was Monday. She could hear yelling in the halls outside her office. She waited until the bell rang and the halls were quiet. Then she took the card from her purse and dialed Ms. Dawson's number at House of Hope.

"Penelope here."

"Ms. Dawson, my name is Bobbie Strickland. I'm Dar-lene Strickland's mother. I understand that you're her case-worker."

"Strickland? Strickland? Oh, yes. She's new here. She's the one whose little girl will be joining us. She showed me her picture. Darling girl. I'm glad you called. As you know, familial involvement is very important to the rehabilitation process. In fact, I'd like to get you involved in our counsel-ing sessions. Is Thursday night good for you?"

"Well, Ms. Dawson, I don't think—"

"Please, call me Penelope."

"Okay—"

"So we'll see you on Thursday? The sessions are held here at the House of Hope. You have the address, right?"

"Yes. I mean, no. I won't be there Thursday. And Monika won't be joining you. That's what I called to tell you. Monika lives with me. And she will continue to live with me."

"Mrs. Strickland, I don't think you understand. Here at—"

The door slammed open, and a large woman wearing a too-tight jersey pantset and $200 worth of blond braids marched toward her desk, with Bobbie's secretary on her heels.

"Bitch, I done tol' you—"

"We will *not* tolerate that kind of language in our school," the secretary said in as official a tone as she could muster. "I'm going to call campus security."

The woman turned around and gave her a threatening look.

"Shuddup, bitch." She turned back to Bobbie. "You da one I come to see."

Bobbie had covered the phone receiver with her hand. She stood and waved the secretary away.

"Ms. Dawson, I'm going to have to call you back," she said into the phone, then hung it up. "Have a seat, ma'am," Bobbie said as she sat.

"It's *Miz* Thompson to you."

"All right, *Miz* Thompson, have a seat."

"I don't have to have no seat. You people—"

"No, you don't *have* to have a seat. But if we're sitting here having a conversation when security arrives, it's more likely I can convince them to go on about their business." The calm look on Bobbie's face belied her inner feelings.

The woman hesitated, blowing out angry breaths, until Bobbie's words sank in. Then she reluctantly settled in the chair and crossed her legs.

"I ain't gon' have these white motherfuckers—"

"Which white motherfuckers?" Bobbie's language clearly caught Ms. Thompson off guard, as Bobbie had intended, but just for an instant.

"That Mr. Gibson. DeShawn say he the one that pulled his arm outta socket. And I want to know what you gonna do about it."

"When did this happen?"

"You know damn well it was last Thursday."

"How did DeShawn tell you it happened?"

"What you mean?" the woman asked defiantly.

"I mean, how did DeShawn say it happened? Did he say that Mr. Gibson just walked up to him and pulled his arm out of its socket?"

"He say he wasn't doing nothing, just talking to his friends."

"So I guess he didn't tell you that he had Jeffery on the ground, about to hit him in his face with a large rock?"

"Oh, I see what's going on here. You just gon' take up for him. You gon' try to smooth it all over." Ms. Thompson stood up. "Your Oreo ass can just talk to my lawyer."

Bobbie kept the calm look on her face and said nothing. She wanted to say, "Your lawyer can just get in line behind Darlene's lawyer."

Ms. Thompson walked to the door and snatched it open. The uniformed security officer looked startled, with his hand still in the air poised to knock. He gave Bobbie a questioning look, but she waved him away. He stood aside and let Ms. Thompson pass. Then, maintaining a little distance between them, he followed her out of the reception area.

Bobbie sighed, then pulled the file out of her drawer. It

contained the incident report she'd asked Bill Gibson to write, her notes, and DeShawn's disciplinary record. How many times had she told Bill to keep his hands off the children? Inwardly she agreed with him that children needed to be touched and held, but in these times, the rules prohibited it. Still, some situations just demand it. Was this one of them? If what he and Jeffery said was true, Bill had had no choice. On the other hand, DeShawn denied that he had a rock, or that there was an argument. And his friends backed up his version. One side, all-white; the other, all-black. On one side, an adult who refused to follow her instructions and had taken every opportunity to undermine her authority to the other teachers. On the other, three boys with less than stellar records.

When the incident had occurred last Thursday, she had been downtown in an interview with the area superintendent for the principalship of the new magnet school. She didn't even find out about it until Friday afternoon when Mrs. Brown sent DeShawn to the office on a referral for cursing at her. He was compiling a record that would soon require that Bobbie institute proceedings to remove him to the alternative school. She hated that aspect of her job more than any other. It seemed it was always black boys being removed from school. There was just something about fourth grade.

While DeShawn was complaining that Mrs. Brown was picking on him, he'd added, "Just like Mr. Gibson. Always picking on me." He didn't mention anything about his arm being out of socket. Hadn't even complained of soreness.

Later, she had called Bill in and questioned him about it. His description of the incident completely justified his actions, but indicated a level of seriousness that should have required him to report it to her. After all, it was her campus. She was responsible for everything that went on there. She was pissed. She'd handed him a pen and a tablet and demanded that he write a report right there. He was pissed. She didn't care. Reading it over now, she wondered whether he had shaded the truth.

By noon, Bobbie had a headache. When she'd been promoted to principal, she hadn't anticipated days like this one. She found Mrs. Brown in the teachers' lounge. No, DeShawn hadn't said anything on Thursday or Friday about his arm hurting. No, Mrs. Brown hadn't observed the incident. No, the other kids weren't talking about it. No, Mr. Gibson hadn't mentioned it to her.

Then Bobbie went to Mrs. Washington's classroom door and asked her to step outside. No, Jeffery hadn't told her anything about an incident. But he was a quiet child who kept to himself. He didn't even take up with the only other white child in the class. But maybe because that child was a girl. Jeffery had transferred in late in the semester, when his mother had moved into a low-income apartment complex in the area. No, Mr. Gibson hadn't mentioned it to her.

When Bobbie returned to her office, she had two messages, one from the Austin Police Department, and one from the hospital. Rubbing her temples, she called the hospital first. The doctor wanted to know if she'd made a decision. She told him she had. When she called the police number, they answered, "Victim Services." They understood she was the next of kin. Was she the one responsible for Mrs. Swink's house? Did she want the number of a service that handled cleanup of homicide scenes?

By the time Bobbie picked Monee up and headed for the hospital, her eyebrows were nearly touching each other. Even Monee couldn't cheer her up. She made Monee sit in the waiting room and do her homework, while she went in to see Mrs. Swink. She looked just as bad as before. Bobbie took a comb from her purse and combed Mrs. Swink's hair as best she could, working around the tubes and bandages.

Night had long fallen by the time Bobbie got home. With the mail tucked under her arm, she turned her key in the door and pushed it open, dropping a piece of mail. She stooped to pick up the card that had fallen on the floor, and a little smile came to her face when she recognized it. She flipped it over and saw the message written in crisp letters: "I brought your drawer by. Sorry I missed you." She looked at her watch as she prodded Monee to get ready for bed. She shouldn't have kept the child out this late on a school night, but what choice did she have? Was it too late to call Ray? She wondered if he was a night owl. Would she seem too forward calling at this hour? She decided to call tomorrow and stuck the card in her purse.

Tuesday was another long day. It had ended with a faculty meeting where Bobbie shared the new directives from administration about the importance of the TAAS test, and the implicit threat of what would happen if the school was on the low-performing list again this year. The teachers stared at her in mute resentment. She shared their feelings. She knew what little they had to work with, and how hard they tried, here at ground zero. She knew that every one of them had at least one child in the class who came to school hungry every day; another child who was in foster care because of parental neglect; another who still suffered the aftereffects of a crack-addicted birth. But she was the principal and it was her job to be the messenger, cheerleader, and taskmaster. The only good thing about her day was that Bill had stayed way away from her.

As soon as the meeting was over, she dashed to her car to pick up Monee, then went straight to the hospital. The newness of the hospital had worn off for Monee, and she was petulant about not being allowed to take the Mandy rag doll to Mrs. Swink. She wouldn't let Bobbie take it to her and protested being left alone in the waiting room. There really wasn't anything Bobbie could do for Mrs. Swink anyway, so they left earlier than the night before.

At home, Bobbie took the leftover gumbo out of the freezer and thawed it in the microwave for a quick meal. As soon as they were done, she insisted that Monee take a bath, since she'd let her get away with a wash-off the night before. Bobbie was drying the bowls and spoons when she realized she had no drawer to put the flatware in. She thought of Ray and remembered that she hadn't called him last night. She took the card from her purse and dialed his number.

"Ray Caldwell speaking."

His tone was so snappy, Bobbie almost felt like saluting. Instead, she sat on the chair and eased her left shoe off.

"Hi, Ray. This is Bobbie. I hope it isn't too late to call."

On his end, Ray set the can of stain down, quickly wiped his hands with an old T-shirt, and turned down the volume on his jambox. "No, it's not too late. I was up."

"Are you busy?"

"Well, I'm always busy," he chuckled. "But never too

busy to hear from you. I mean, I was just piddling around here in the shop. I'm glad you called." He leaned back against his workbench, a smile on his face. "I think I've fixed your drawer so that it'll work for a while." Ray knew that he'd fixed it so well that her whole house would fall down before that drawer broke again. In fact, he'd built another drawer of real wood and attached the old facing to it.

"I hope it didn't take too much of your time," Bobbie said, massaging her foot.

"Nah, I found some pieces around here in my shop. No trouble at all. You sound tired."

Bobbie exhaled. "I am. But I didn't want you to think . . . I wanted you to know that I got your message."

"Home Center is still open. I don't guess you'd be up to looking at cabinets tonight, would you?"

"Lord, no. As soon as Monee gets out of the tub, I'm going to soak this old body, then crawl into bed."

"I guess it is kind of late for that anyway for a weeknight. And you can't take Monee out in the night air after her bath. How about Saturday, then?"

"Are you sure you want to do that? I told you I can't afford new cabinets. It would just be a waste of your time."

"How about you let me decide what to do with my time, Miss Boss Lady. I've kind of gotten in the habit since I left the army." A smile played around his mouth. A smile played around hers too.

"Well . . ."

"So Saturday it is. I'll pick you up around three."

"Three is okay. I've got to go. Monee's calling me."

Ray hung up the phone, the smile still on his face. He didn't get to talk to her as long as he'd wanted, but he had at least gotten her to agree to go look at the cabinets. He was looking forward to Saturday.

"Coming, Monee," Bobbie called out. She pushed off her other shoe, picked them both up, and padded up the stairs in her stocking feet. She didn't feel nearly as tired Saturday.

When Bobbie picked Monee up from school on Wednesday, Monee was cranky and out of sorts.

"Granny, I don't want to go to the hospital."

"Monee, don't even start that. I don't want to go either, but I have to. Mrs. Swink doesn't have anybody else but me to see about her."

"Us, Granny. She has us. But if you won't let me see her, why do I have to go?" Monee whined. "Why can't I just stay at home?"

"Because you're too young to stay home alone. And because I said so."

"But, Granny, I want to see her. And I brought the Mandy doll for her again."

Bobbie's impulse was to say, "Don't make me stop this car." That threat would have brought immediate compliance from Darby or Darlene. But not this child. Maybe she wasn't as strict with Monee as she'd been with her own because she was older now and had a better understanding of what was really important. Maybe she was trying to make up for what was missing in Monee's life. Maybe she just didn't have the energy. Instead of the threat, she said, "We'll see."

When they got to ICU, Bobbie hesitated. She looked

down at Monee. They both knew Bobbie was going to relent.

"Now, Monee, I'm going to take you in. But you can only stay for a minute. Mrs. Swink isn't going to look like herself. I don't want you to be frightened."

"I'm not scared, Granny."

Bobbie opened the door and they walked into the brightly lit room. Monitoring equipment was mounted on the wall above each of the four beds, with IV and oxygen tubes connected to four patients. A workstation and a stool were next to each bed. Mrs. Swink was in the second bed from the door. A nurse was at the last bed. She nodded to Bobbie, then spying Monee, rushed over to them.

"Children aren't allowed in ICU. You'll have to take her out."

Monee spoke up in a small voice. "I just want to give Mrs. Swink this doll. She'll make her feel better." Monee held it up for the nurse to see.

The stern look on the nurse's face slowly softened. "Well, only for just a minute. That's all. Else you'll get me in trouble."

Monee nodded that she understood, then looked around until she saw Mrs. Swink. A shocked look skittered across her face, then she put on her "big girl" face. She slowly walked over to the bed, then turned back to Bobbie.

"Can I touch her, Granny?"

Bobbie nodded. The nurse said in a quiet voice, "You can touch her. You can even talk to her. She can't talk back. But I believe my patients can hear you, so be careful what you say." With that, the nurse walked two patients over and busied herself with papers at the workstation.

Monee stood silently, close to the bed. The slow and steady blip from the heart monitor was all she could hear. She jerked when the blood pressure cuff automatically tightened on Mrs. Swink's thin arm. Monee held her breath until it released with a quiet swoosh. She tentatively touched Mrs. Swink's hand, then quickly drew hers back. Then she put her little hand over the frail, wrinkled one and held it there. She leaned down close to Mrs. Swink's ear and whispered something in a voice so low that Bobbie couldn't hear. Monee stood back, fully expecting Mrs. Swink to wake up. Then a look of disappointment covered her face. She leaned over again and whispered in Mrs. Swink's ear. Then she raised the wrinkled hand and nestled the soft doll under her forearm. She patted her hand and smiled. Then she looked up at Bobbie.

"She's gonna wake up, Granny. I know she is. She's gonna be just like she used to. And she's gonna bake me some more of her big tea cakes." Monee's face brimmed with confidence.

Bobbie nodded and turned her face away so that Monee couldn't see the tears that had welled up in her eyes. She realized that Monee had more faith about it than she had.

"Come on, Monee. Let's go. We don't want to get the nurse in trouble. She's been nice to us." Monee took the hand Bobbie held out and turned back to the nurse to wave.

Just as they reached the door, the nurse's sudden movement caught Bobbie's eye before the change in frequency of the heart monitor blips registered in her ear. The nurse rushed over to Mrs. Swink's bed.

8

"TAKE THE child out. Now!" the nurse ordered over her shoulder.

Bobbie grabbed Monee's hand, and they both took one halfhearted step backward, as though to comply.

The nurse checked the paper tape that continuously fed from the EKG. She checked all the connections on the lines that ran to the monitor. She took a little flashlight out of her pocket, raised Mrs. Swink's eyelid, and shone the light in one eye, then the other. In between, she jotted notes on the chart. She was oblivious to Bobbie and Monee's presence.

Without making a sound, Monee inched sideways until she gained a view of Mrs. Swink's face. When one of Mrs. Swink's eyes slowly opened, then the other, Monee squeezed Bobbie's hand. Bobbie looked down at Monee and saw her confident "I told you" look. They both looked back at Mrs. Swink.

A dazed look was on Mrs. Swink's face, and her eyes

rolled upward. Her lids closed, then slowly opened again. There was no light of recognition of the nurse leaning over her. She reached for the tube that was in her mouth, but the nurse stayed her hand and said something in a soothing tone. That seemed to calm the old lady a little. Her eyes closed again for a few seconds, then opened. She looked around. When her eyes found Monee, a little grimace of a smile came to her lips around the tube.

Saturday was quiet in the hospital. Bobbie sat in the chair, staring into nothing on the pale green wall of the tiny room. Mrs. Swink dozed peacefully in the bed next to her. After another day of observation in ICU, Mrs. Swink had been moved to this room. Bobbie hadn't even tried to persuade Monee that Mrs. Swink's awakening had not been her doing. In the back of her mind, even *she* was willing to believe it.

Mrs. Swink hadn't recovered exactly. She still looked a fright, but she was so much better. She could talk a little, but not long. And a lot of what she said didn't make sense. The nurses told Bobbie that it wasn't unusual for a patient who had withstood an ordeal like hers to be a little confused. It reminded Bobbie of the way her dad had been just after his stroke three years ago. It also reminded her that she hadn't talked to him in the week since Mrs. Swink's beating. She stepped into the hall and pulled her phone from her purse.

"Darby? What are you doing home this time of day? You're not skipping class, are you? You can't afford to slack off now, Darby. This is your last semester and you know—"

"I assure you, Mama, that come June, I will be Dr. Darby

Strickland, DDS. So put your mind at rest and quit already with the big-mama thing. I took a break from my lab today and came home to have lunch with Grampa. He's getting depressed again and won't eat sometimes."

Bobbie gave a tired sigh and rubbed her forehead with her index and middle fingers, using her thumb as a brace at her temple. "Do I need to come to Houston?"

"Naw. I got it covered. He's about a stubborn old cuss, but I can usually coax him to eat. Actually, I threaten to take him over to the dental school and pull the rest of his teeth, then force-feed him through a tube and—"

"Darby! I'm driving down there tomorrow. Don't you—"

"Just kidding, Mama. Chill. I bring him the kind of greasy burger he loves about once a week, so he can have a break from those Meals-On-Wheels lunches. He's a sucker for a good greasy burger."

Bobbie calmed herself. Darby had always been a big teaser, so she shouldn't have fallen for it. But he was her responsible child, the one she could depend on.

"Darby, I don't know what I'd do without you. I can't say thank you enough for moving in with Dad, and especially just when you were starting school. I just—"

"No problem, Mama. Where else could a guy get free rent and leftover Meals-On-Wheels lunches?"

"Can I talk to Dad?" Bobbie leaned back against the wall in anticipation of a nice long chat.

"You want me to wake him up? He's taking a little nap. But I can get him for you."

"No, baby, that's fine. Just tell him I called. I'm at the hospital with Mrs. Swink—"

"Mrs. Swink? Is she okay?"

"Somebody broke in her house and beat her up pretty bad. It was touch-and-go for a few days, but she's coming along. I think she's gonna be all right. It'll just take time."

"Damn. When did this happen?"

"Last Friday night."

"Wonder why Darlene didn't mention it. Does she know? Have you seen her?"

"You talked to Darlene? When?"

"She called a couple of days ago."

"Looking for money, I'll bet."

There was silence on the other end of the line, and Bobbie knew what that meant.

"She's my sister, Mama," he finally said. "How's little Monee?"

"That's another thing I need to tell you—" Bobbie felt a presence and turned to see the doctor standing next to her with an expectant look on his face. "Look, Darby, I've got to go. The doctor is here. I'll call you back."

Bobbie fought hard to keep the disgusted look off her face while she listened to the doctor. Now he was positive that Mrs. Swink would recover, but they could do no more for her in this setting. Bobbie needed to find a suitable placement for Mrs. Swink so he could discharge her: "You know, with Medicare limits and all." He pressed Bobbie to immediately find a nursing home or an assisted-living facility. And to think, not a week ago, he had wanted to assist her death.

Bobbie spent the rest of the day looking for a "suitable placement." One nursing home tour was all she could stand. Then she took the guided tour of four of the seven assisted-living centers that the hospital social worker had told her about. Slick brochures littered the front seat of her car, along with Monee's junk. Autumn Oaks was the only one that had an apartment available immediately. As an added bonus, it was on the route between her house and school. She sent up a silent prayer of thanks.

Back at the hospital, she explained the situation to Mrs. Swink.

"Couldn't I just stay with you, Bobbie? I'd try not to be any trouble."

"I've already thought about that, Mrs. Swink. But you know all of my bedrooms are upstairs. You couldn't climb those stairs two years ago. You know you can't do it now." Bobbie thought about the loose stairwell post and shook her head. "Autumn Oaks is really nice. And they have a nurse twenty-four hours a day. And they will bring your meals until you're strong enough to go to the dining room. And it's close to the house, so I could see about you."

"Autumn Oaks? Sounds like a place one goes to die."

"Aw, Mrs. Swink. It's not like that."

"Why not Spring Oaks? Or Summer Oaks?"

Bobbie shrugged her shoulders. "I don't know much about oaks. I just thought it was a nice name."

"Humph. I'll just go home. To my house."

Bobbie stared at her a long time. "How would you manage? You can hardly stand up."

"I can manage. I've managed all these years."

Bobbie pondered that again. Earlier in the day on the drive between centers, she'd called a couple of the home-health-care agencies the social worker had told her about, from her cell phone. The cost for eight hours a day was twice the cost of the assisted-living center.

"You can't manage by yourself now. If it were summer, it would be different. I could take care of you. But I have to go to work. And we don't have time to wait. The doctor wants to discharge you as soon as he can. Like tomorrow. This is really best."

"Best for whom?"

"Best for you, Mrs. Swink."

Mrs. Swink let out a long sigh and closed her eyes. She didn't say anything for so long Bobbie thought she'd fallen asleep. And Bobbie hadn't even gotten to the hard question.

"You think this dying place is really best, Bobbie?"

"Yeah. For now."

"How long is 'for now'?"

Bobbie looked at the wounds on Mrs. Swink's face, the places where her hair had been shaved, the plastic brace on her arm.

"Would you do it for thirty days? Then we'll see."

"You know my Zeke is a railroad man. You remember my Zeke, don't you?"

Bobbie was caught short by that. Of course she knew that. Mrs. Swink had told her a thousand times. But Zeke had been dead over thirty years when she met Mrs. Swink.

"Gone for a month at a time. All over Texas. Laying that track. Moving those big timbers. Me and Mandy just occupy ourselves till he comes back." Mrs. Swink smoothed the doll's hair over and over. "Thirty days is so long. How will he know where I am?"

"Well . . ." Bobbie didn't know what to say.

"When he comes back. How will he know where I am?"

Bobbie was torn. Should she try to bring Mrs. Swink back to reality? She didn't know where that would lead. She took the short course.

"It's not that long. I think Zeke would want you to be safe. And if I see him, I'll tell him where you are." Mrs. Swink seemed satisfied with that, as evidenced by the relieved smile that came to her face. Bobbie exhaled.

"Will this Autumn Oaks cost much?" Mrs. Swink asked.

"Ah, well, yes. But don't you worry about that. We'll figure something out."

"Well, that's no problem, Bobbie. I've got a little money tucked away. And Zeke always brings me his money. He isn't a drinking and carousing kind of man."

A little money wasn't gonna cut this cake, Bobbie thought. But she'd already decided. She would pay the first month's rent out of her own savings. She owed Mrs. Swink that. That would give her thirty days to figure out what to do.

At nine, Bobbie put her key in her door. When she pushed it open, a card fell to the floor. She picked it up, read it, then smacked herself on the forehead. She'd forgotten all about Ray and the cabinets, in all her rushing about looking at living centers, then going back to the hospital, then back to the center to sign the lease, then calling movers. The least she could do was call. The phone rang only once before he picked up.

"Ray? This is Bobbie. I'm so sorry. I just forgot." She had the phone clamped between her ear and shoulder as she pushed her shoes off, then sorted through the mail.

"Forgot? I guess I didn't make much of an impression on you."

"Oh, Ray. I was busy. You won't believe the day I've had. I just—"

"Busy?"

She heard thinly disguised irritation in his voice. That irritated her.

"Yes. Busy. Too busy to think about some . . . cabinets. I have a lot going on. Listen, I gotta go. When things settle down, I'll call and see if we can reschedule."

Bobbie hung up the phone, her mood grown foul. Tossing the mail on the counter, she entirely missed the letter with a return address of an attorney's office. Upstairs, she fell across the bed, exhausted. She lay on her back, staring at the ceiling, trying to figure out how she could get at least Mrs. Swink's bed to the room at Autumn Oaks. She could take Mrs. Swink's rocking chair in her car, but not a bed or a dresser. If she could get those things, that would be enough for now. She could arrange for the rest of the furniture later.

Ray hung up the phone after the line went dead. What had he said? Why was she pissed off? *He* was the one who'd been stood up. And he'd been so pumped about it. How could she just forget their date? Maybe it wasn't a date in her mind the way that it was in his. Maybe she had another man. Then it came to him. And he was ashamed. He hadn't even asked about her neighbor. He grabbed his keys and jacket.

Thirty minutes later, he stood on Bobbie's porch. He gingerly held the hot box balanced on his fingertips in one hand and rang the bell with the other. He squeezed his eyes shut when the bright porch light came on. When the door opened, he wore a sheepish smile.

"I thought you might be hungry. I thought you might have been too busy to eat."

Bobbie crooked her head. How did he know she hadn't eaten since the bowl of cereal this morning?

"A couple of brothers have a little restaurant not too far from my house. They fry some mean catfish."

Hunger rumbled through Bobbie's stomach. And it was stronger than the annoyance she felt.

"I could leave it. I just wanted to apologize."

Bobbie pushed the screen door open. "That box looks too big for just me. Monee's staying with a friend. Come on in. Have you eaten?"

This time she didn't even care about the dolls and toys strewn about.

"How's Mrs. Swink doing?" Ray asked, following her to the kitchen.

As she set the table, Bobbie sighed. "She's holding her own. No. In fact, she's better. She's in a room now. She still looks real bad. But I guess she's as well as the hospital is going to get her. The rest will just take time. The doctor wants to kick her out of the hospital. I spent the whole day looking for a place for her. That's why I forgot about the cabinets. But I found a place. She wants to go back to her own house, but this is better. At least until she's able to take care of herself. And it's close. Easy for me to see about her in the meantime."

"Is there anything I can do to help you?"

Bobbie stopped and looked at him. "What I really need is somebody to move some furniture. Like, tomorrow."

Ray swallowed a bite of catfish. "I can move furniture. How much furniture?"

"Well, I figure if I can get a bed and a dresser, that would be enough to get her settled in. That's the crisis part. All the movers I called needed a week's notice, a month's notice. I've got to get a bed, at least, there tomorrow. I found a place where I can rent a roll-away bed, but they can't deliver it for a week."

"Well, I could move a bed. Maybe a dresser too, if I had a little help."

"Could you really? I could help."

Ray laughed. "It would have to be a pretty small dresser."

"If you've got time, we can go down to her house. Then you could see."

Bobbie held the key to Mrs. Swink's house lightly in her hand. It felt good walking with Ray. But she hoped Idalia wasn't watching out her window. Busybody. The neighborhood was quiet. When they reached the porch, Ray caught her arm and held her back. She looked at him, questioning. He put his index finger to his mouth, signaling her to be quiet. She stood stock-still. Through the lace curtains, she could see the faint beam of a flashlight inside. She didn't know what to do. She looked back at Ray and he pulled her back to the tree in the middle of the yard.

"Stay here," he whispered. Then he eased up on the porch and peered in the window.

Bobbie watched him ease back off the porch. He motioned her to stay by the tree, then he sneaked around the side of the house. She looked across the street toward

Idalia's house, but it was dark. In fact, all the surrounding houses were dark. She nervously worried the fingers of one hand in her other hand. The seconds ticking by felt like minutes, then hours. She thought about going around to the back of the house, but Ray had told her to stay there by the tree. She could run to Idalia's and pound on the door until she roused her. But what could Idalia do? They could call the police. That would take too long. She had to do something. She took tentative steps toward the side yard. The gate was closed. Ray must have scaled it. She couldn't. She could fiddle it open during the day, but not in the dark. Still, she felt she had to try. She'd just have to be quiet about it. She felt the contraption of rope, latches, and springs that Mrs. Swink had made, trying to remember the secret to it, so that she could do it quietly. Just as she felt it release and the gate swung open, she heard a loud crash. Glass showered the air as a dark figure catapulted through the window. She stifled a scream as the figure rolled on the ground, gained footing, and ran straight toward her, head bowed in tackle mode. Suddenly, another figure jumped out of the window, flinging more glass outward. Before she could react, she took the brunt of the charge in her stomach. The air whooshed out of her and she sprawled on the ground flat on her back.

9

WHEN BOBBIE came to, Ray was patting her cheek and calling her name. His voice sounded hollow and distant. She had thought only cartoon characters saw stars when they got knocked out, but she couldn't deny the ones she was seeing. She shook her head to clear it and strained to bring her eyes into focus. She gasped for breath and blinked her eyes. Ray pulled her into a sitting position. When she swooned, he sat next to her and steadied her by putting his arm around her shoulder.

"Breathe, Bobbie. Just breathe."

Slowly, her head cleared. She remembered the dark figure charging toward her, but she didn't remember much after that. "What happened? Are you okay?"

"Better than you," he said.

She picked his hand up and saw trickles of blood where the glass had cut him.

"Who was it? I guess you didn't catch them?"

"Nah. He got too much of a lead on me."

Lights came on at the house next door, and Mrs. Downs peered around the edge of her porch. "Who's there?" she asked, her thin, reedy voice full of suspicion and false bravado.

"Ray Caldwell."

"Who?" she asked in the same tone.

"It's me. Bobbie. From down the street. Call the police."

"What's going on over there, Bobbie?"

"Someone was in Mrs. Swink's house. Call the police."

"Can you stand up?" Ray asked, offering his hand.

Bobbie nodded and he pulled her to her feet. "Let's go in the house. Where's the key?"

Bobbie handed the key to him and he helped her to the porch.

Inside, Bobbie turned on the lights. The living room appeared to be in order. Same with the dining room, except that all the drawers and doors to the hutch were open. In the kitchen all the cabinet doors were open and the contents of the drawers were on the countertop.

"Can you tell if anything is missing?" Ray asked.

Bobbie just shrugged her shoulders. It was hard to tell from the mess. In the hallway, she reached down, picked up the flashlight, and turned it off.

"You shouldn't have done that," Ray said. "There might have been fingerprints."

Bobbie looked at her fingers closed around the flashlight, then shrugged in resignation.

When they got to the bedroom, everything was in disarray. Bobbie remembered that she hadn't called the number for the cleaning service that the homicide detective had given her. Now she wished she had. When she saw dark splotches of dried blood on the floor, she refused to enter the room.

"Looks like there was quite a fight here," Ray said.

Bobbie thought of the black-and-blue places on Mrs. Swink's face and arms and had to turn away.

"Do you know whether she kept money around the house?"

Bobbie knew, not only because she wrote out the checks for Mrs. Swink to sign, but also because she went to the bank for the monthly $350 withdrawal. She had cautioned her against keeping so much cash, but Mrs. Swink always said, "If someone comes to rob me, I'd rather have a little something to give 'em than get beat up or killed for nothing." Bobbie glanced at the funeral-home calendar on the wall in the hallway. Since it was only the tenth of the month, she knew there would have been a couple of hundred dollars in the house. Bobbie went to the desk near the front door. She found an envelope marked *Paperboy* with $18 in it. There was one marked *Cable,* but it was empty. Another marked *Yardman* with $35 in it. She thought of Mrs. Swink's system for keeping up with her money and vowed to remember it when the time came that she wasn't as sharp as she was now.

"Look what I found," Ray said, stepping into the living room. He held up a small hardcover book. "It was on the table by her bed."

Bobbie looked at the title—*The Mis-Education of the Negro*—then at Ray with a quizzical frown. "You haven't read that?"

He flipped open the cover and held it at a slant. Bobbie's

eyebrows raised as she walked toward him. "So she got beat up for nothing. I wonder why she didn't just give 'em the money." Bobbie took the bills out of the hole cut in the book and counted them. "There's over two thousand dollars here."

"I know," Ray answered. "Twenty-four hundred to be exact. I don't know how they didn't find it. That room is torn up pretty bad."

"You know the old saying—hide it in a book."

Ray gave a wry twist of his lips. "Who would have thunk. Wonder how she made the hole in the pages."

"She has a little pair of embroidery scissors. They look like some kind of exotic bird, or a swan or something. And even though her hands are a little shaky, she can really work with them. I'll bet she cut the pages with them."

"Shouldn't the police be here by now?" Ray asked. "You think the neighbor called?"

"I'm sure she did, but you're right, they should have been here by now. I'm going to call again."

When Bobbie hung up the phone, she turned to Ray. "They said since the intruder is no longer here and no one is in danger, we can go to the station tomorrow and make a report."

"They should come take prints or something."

Bobbie shrugged. "Since they're not coming, I'd just as soon go home."

"You'd better take the book with you. My guess is that whoever was here was looking for it. They may come back. Lock the door."

"What difference does it make? The window's all broken out."

"I'll come by early in the morning and put some ply-board over it. The wooden frame is broken and that will take some time to repair."

"What about the dresser? Did you get a look at it?"

"Oh, yeah. I'm gonna need some help with that. And it's too heavy for you to lift."

"I'll see if Jimbo can help you in the morning. What time?"

"I'm an early riser. So whenever he can help will be fine with me."

When they reached the front door, Bobbie stopped. "Just a minute. I'm going to set a timer on the lamp. Just so it will look like Mrs. Swink is here."

As they walked back down the street, Ray put his arm around Bobbie's shoulder. She felt comforted. And com-fortable. How long had it been since a man had put his arm on her in a way that didn't contain an expectation? She couldn't remember that there had ever been such a time. And there had never been a time a man had jumped out a window for her or chased a bad guy for her.

At her door, she wanted to invite him in. But she wasn't sure what kind of message that would send. Monee wouldn't be home, so the house would be quiet. She had looked forward to a little peace and quiet. But now, nagging at the back of her mind, there was an element of fear that was foreign to her. She hadn't lived with a man since she'd been an adult. She'd always had to fend for herself, so being scared was something she couldn't indulge. She'd just have to deal with it. Her whole life, she'd always had to just deal with it. So it surprised her when she found herself saying, "Why don't you come in. Let me see about those cuts."

After she'd locked the front door behind them, she said, "All of my first-aid stuff is in the upstairs cabinet. I'll be right back."

In the bathroom she held his hand under warm running water. After she'd poured hydrogen peroxide over his hand, she placed gauze over it and secured it with adhesive tape.

"I'm not much of a nurse, but I do get to deal with minor injuries at school when the nurse is at the other campus. This is the best I can do. I'm so sorry this happened."

"It's not your fault. I just wish I'd caught that joker. He'd be in a world of hurt now."

"What happened?"

"When I went around the side of the house, the window was open. I could see that someone was in the other room, so I climbed through the window. When I got to the hall-way, I could see him. Tall fellow. He was going through the drawers. But just as I was easing up on him, I stepped on something on the floor and the sound startled him. He charged me. We struggled, but he got loose and ran for the window like a wild man. It was stupid of me, but I knew you were outside. Before I knew it, I had charged out the window too. I guess it was all that adrenaline. Anyway, I'll bet he's more cut up than I am. He took the brunt of the glass."

"What did he look like?"

"Can't tell you. Just tall. Black guy. He shined the light in my face, just before he charged me."

"So he knows what you look like."

"Hard to say. It all happened so fast. But, yeah, probably."

10

BOBBIE DIDN'T want to miss church again, but there
was no way around it, with Mrs. Swink being discharged
from the hospital at 10 A.M. She helped Mrs. Swink into the
car, being careful not to jar the arm with the splint on it. She
hoped that Mrs. Swink would like the apartment. It was only
a one-bedroom, but south-facing windows in both rooms
made it light and airy. Earlier that morning, Ray and Jimbo
had moved enough of her furniture to completely furnish it.
Bobbie had selected the pieces that Mrs. Swink would really
want and that would make her feel most at home. The nightstand and dresser from the bedroom, the sofa, coffee table,
and rocking chair from the living room. And the curio cabinet. Bobbie had been reluctant to move so many pieces, only
to have to move them back in thirty days, but Ray had
insisted that it would be no trouble. Bobbie felt a sense of
pride in how comfortable the apartment looked, even down
to the doilies on the arms of the overstuffed couch.

When they arrived, an attendant rushed out to the car with a wheelchair. At first Mrs. Swink refused to sit in it. But Bobbie's insistence and the weakness of her body from days in bed overcame Mrs. Swink's stubbornness, so she acquiesced. "Hand me my baby," she said.

Mrs. Swink hadn't let the Mandy doll out of her sight since she'd regained consciousness, and she treated it like a real child. She'd even buckled it in the seat belt. Bobbie's brow knitted in worry. Maybe the confusion would pass in a few more days, she thought. She hoped. Bobbie reached back in the front seat of the car, retrieved the doll, and laid it carefully in Mrs. Swink's lap.

As they passed through the lobby, Mrs. Swink held her head high, avoiding the curious stares of the other residents. Bobbie smiled and spoke to those who were sitting on couches or pushing walkers. When they reached the door of the apartment, Mrs. Swink insisted on getting out of the wheelchair. She leaned heavily on Bobbie's arm as Bobbie unlocked the door. When they entered, a slight smile crossed her face at the sight of her own furniture. Her eyes watered as she slowly walked around, running her hand over each piece. Bobbie talked nervously, pointing out the features of the apartment—the two-burner stove built into the countertop, the microwave, and the small refrigerator in the minikitchen, the view from the big windows.

"This is really nice." But Mrs. Swink's eyes said, "You know I really don't want to be here."

"I'm glad you like it." But Bobbie's eyes said, "I know. It's the best we can do for now."

"They have twenty-four-hour call service. If you need anything, just call this number." Bobbie held up a card, then put it back by the telephone on the lamp table. "There's one by the phone in the bedroom too. Let's go look in there." She led Mrs. Swink into the other room.

Stepping into the other room, Mrs. Swink stopped at her dresser. She picked up the new picture frame and looked at it a long time. She saw the crimped place in the photo of Zeke and Mandy. Tears ran down her face, past the little smile on her face. She set it back on the dresser and opened a drawer.

"I tried to get everything I thought you'd need," Bobbie said. "But if I missed something you want, just let me know."

Mrs. Swink looked up at her. "You're a good girl, Bobbie. You've done so much for me. How can I thank you?" Then she grabbed the dresser for support.

"How about you lie down for a while. You look a little peaked." Bobbie led her to her bed and helped her in. "I've got to pick Monee up, but I'll be by around five. You just take it easy," Bobbie said as she pulled the cover over her.

Mrs. Swink grabbed Bobbie's hand. "Are you coming back?"

"Sure. As soon as I get Monee a bite to eat. The attendant will bring your dinner here to your room today."

"Will you bring me something from my house?"

"I'll bring whatever you want later in the week." The thought of going in the house again almost made Bobbie cringe. Perhaps Ray would go back with her. "When you feel a little better, you can make a list."

"I've got to have it today. I've got to." Mrs. Swink was struggling up on her elbows.

"Okay, okay. I'll bring it. You just lie back. What is it?"

"I want my Bible."

Bobbie thought the request a little odd since Mrs. Swink

wasn't much of a Bible-thumper. In fact, sometimes, when Mrs. Swink talked of having her husband and child taken from her, Bobbie wondered if she even believed. Maybe the brush with death had changed Mrs. Swink's mind.

"Well, Mrs. Swink, if you just want to read the Bible, there's one in the living room. It's a welcoming present from Autumn Oaks. I'll get it for you now."

When Bobbie returned with the plain black book, Mrs. Swink shook her head. "Not that one. I want my big Bible. The one with the gold-edged pages. It's on the shelf in the living room. I showed you that time. It's got all my dates in it. All my important things."

"Like what? What would you need here?" Bobbie asked, trying to keep any hint of irritation off her face.

Mrs. Swink's face tightened and strained as though she was trying to remember. "Something really important. Just bring it to me. Please, Bobbie."

Bobbie wanted to argue with her, to tell her that the Bible would be safe in her house. Surely no one would steal a Bible. But when she saw the agitated look on Mrs. Swink's face, she sighed and nodded. And added another chore to her list.

Bobbie left Autumn Oaks burdened with a thousand worries. When she pulled up in front of the Masons' house, she thought she would have to reciprocate on the sleepover thing pretty soon. How would she work in a time to entertain a houseful of little girls with everything else on her plate? Mrs. Mason wore a harried look when she opened the door. Bobbie smiled when Monee came down the stairs amid a group of giggling girls. When they got to the car, Monee tossed her overnight bag in the backseat.

"How was your day, sweetheart? Buckle up, now."

"It was fine, Granny. Except for Jennifer. I hate her."

"Don't say that, Monee. What did Jennifer do?"

"She said I couldn't be in her new club because I don't have a daddy," Monee said, pouting.

"Of course you have a daddy. Everybody has a daddy."

"Well, who is my daddy then?" Monee fixed her with a questioning stare.

Bobbie hadn't expected it this soon. She wasn't prepared with an answer. As uncomfortable as it had been with Darlene and Darby, at least she had an answer for them. They knew who their daddy was. She didn't know who Monee's daddy was. Darlene had refused to tell her, and whoever he was, he hadn't stepped forward to claim paternity of the baby. Bobbie had questioned her numerous times, believing that Trey was the culprit, but Darlene always denied it. Now Bobbie passed the buck.

"That's something you need to ask your mother."

A veil descended over Monee's face and Bobbie read a mustard seed of mistrust in it. But what else could she say? And why did she feel so guilty? It wasn't as if she was hiding something that she knew. Yet she didn't want to tell the child the truth—that she didn't know. As much trouble as Darlene had given her and as many disappointments as Darlene had dealt Monee, somehow acknowledging that Bobbie didn't know who Monee's father was would cross a bridge that couldn't be uncrossed, ever. It would say something that couldn't be retracted about Bobbie's relationship with her daughter and would tell Monee something about her mother that couldn't be retracted either.

"Guess what?" Bobbie asked, trying to sound bright and

cheerful. "Mrs. Swink is out of the hospital. She's at a place called Autumn Oaks. That's the big building over on Beale Street. She took the Mandy doll with her." Even as she said it, Bobbie worried again over Mrs. Swink's attachment to the doll and her confusion.

"That's good." Monee stared straight ahead and her voice was expressionless.

"We can go see her after you do your homework."

"Okay." Monee's expression didn't change.

"And guess what else?"

"What?"

"Mr. Caldwell is coming over for dinner tomorrow."

"Why?"

"Because I invited him."

"Why?"

"Well, he and Jimbo moved Mrs. Swink's furniture for me. I thought it would be a nice treat. Just to say thank you and show him I appreciated his help."

"Is Jimbo coming too?"

Bobbie jerked her head to look at Monee. She didn't like the tone of her voice, that edge of challenge. Of course she hadn't invited Jimbo. She had slipped him a $20 bill. That worked for both of them. But she couldn't have given Ray $20. She had halfheartedly offered to pay him for moving the furniture. He'd said he couldn't take any money, but he would take another of her home-cooked meals sometime. Then she'd said, "What about tomorrow night?" Still, she didn't like the tone of Monee's voice.

"No, Jimbo's not coming. He didn't want to come."

★   ★   ★

Monday night, Bobbie was rushing around trying to have everything ready by seven-thirty. Her day at school had been one more day in hell. She'd had to break up two fights on the playground. Bill Gibson had stirred up more trouble among the teachers. He'd changed the playground duty schedule without clearing it with her and had let the teachers believe it was her idea. It had taken her half a day to calm that storm. She'd rushed by to check on Mrs. Swink as soon as she picked Monee up. Monee wanted to stay longer, but Bobbie had to face the after-work crowd at the grocery store to pick up fresh corn for dinner. When they were home, Monee balked at every instruction. She didn't see why she had to take her dolls upstairs. She didn't see why she had to set the dining room table. She didn't see why they couldn't just eat in the kitchen the way they always did. Bobbie caught herself being sharp with her.

"You don't have to see why, missy. Just do it." From the corner of her eye, she even thought she caught Monee rolling her eyes at her.

At seven-thirty, Bobbie was in her bathroom with the tube of lipstick poised in the air. Why was she doing this? She never wore lipstick at home. Well, just a little wouldn't hurt. She ran the big-toothed comb through her hair. Then smoothed on a little gel and patted her hair into place. Should she put on some perfume? Well, just one little spray. Then she thought about changing clothes. She'd been in such a rush to get the dinner started that she'd only taken off her suit jacket. But the skirt and blouse looked so schoolmarmish. She should put on something more casual, she thought. Her new caftan would be perfect. When she turned to go to her closet, she saw Monee standing in the doorway, watching her.

"What do you need, Monee?"

"Nothing. Why can't I watch TV downstairs on the big TV? Why do we have to have the music on?"

"Because I want it to be nice when Mr. Caldwell comes. And you have a television in your room."

"I'm hungry, Granny. Why can't we just go ahead and eat now?"

"Because Mr. Caldwell isn't here yet."

"Can't I just go ahead and eat? I want to eat in the kitchen anyway."

"No, Monee. We are all going to eat in the dining room. He'll be here any minute."

"But you said seven-thirty," Monee said, pouting. "Maybe he's not coming."

Bobbie looked at the clock radio on the shelf: 7:45. Was he standing her up? Had he forgotten? Had she gone to all this trouble for nothing? Maybe she should call him. No, too anxious. Yes. After all, if he wasn't coming, she could put on her pj's instead and they could go ahead and eat. When she reached the phone, the message light was on. She pressed the button and was relieved to hear his voice.

"Bobbie, Ray here. Something came up. I'm going to be a little late, but I'm on the way. I hope it's not too much of an inconvenience."

Just then the doorbell chimed.

11

RAY STOOD on the porch, a vase filled with pink carnations in his hand. "I'm sorry I'm late. I brought you these." He handed her the vase of flowers.

"You shouldn't have." But the smile on her face said she was glad he had. Bobbie couldn't remember a man, other than her father, giving her flowers. When the babies were born, he had brought a big bouquet of red carnations to her hospital room. Even before his stroke, John Strickland was a man of few words. He doted on his only child and there wasn't a prouder man on earth when she was awarded a full scholarship to college.

Although he hadn't said a word at breakfast the morning after she'd told her mama that she was pregnant, she had seen the disappointment on his face and he avoided eye contact with her. The night before, she'd heard the hushed conversation through the walls separating their bedrooms. She couldn't make out the words, but she could hear the anger and sorrow in her mother's voice. She heard her mother's sobbing. She didn't hear his voice at all. Over the months until the twins' birth, she'd watched his expression go from disappointment to resignation to defeat. But, in the end, when she'd felt most alone, he'd brought her carnations. And now Ray had.

"They're beautiful. Thank you. Come on in," Bobbie said, stepping back from the door.

"I had to make a delivery and the buyer just wanted to talk on and on and on."

"That's all right, what I fixed isn't time-sensitive. Come on this way, we're eating in the dining room." She turned to the stairwell and called, "Monee, come on down. It's time for dinner. Mr. Caldwell is here." Bobbie set the vase of flowers in the center of the table. They matched her draperies and she wondered if he had chosen the color with that in mind. "Why don't you have a seat. Would you like something to drink?"

"I'm starving. I believe I would rather save the drink for after dinner."

"That's fine. I think that would be better. I'll be right back with the food."

Before going in the kitchen, Bobbie called out to Monee again. Bobbie returned with a casserole dish, then made two more trips for the other dishes. A delicate hint of rosemary filled the dining room. "Where is that girl?" she said irritably. "I'll be right back."

Bobbie climbed the stairs and found Monee in her room stretched out across the bed. "Didn't you hear me calling you?"

Monee didn't move. "I'm not hungry."

"Oh, no, ma'am. You were starving just a little while ago. You come on downstairs."

"I don't want to. Can't I just go to bed?"

"You can go to bed right after you eat. Now come on downstairs."

"But I don't wanna eat, Granny," Monee whined. "My stomach is hurting."

"You didn't say anything about this before." Bobbie thought about her food, cooling on the table.

"But it hurts, Granny."

Monee sounded so pitiful that Bobbie almost believed her. "Where does it hurt?"

"Right here," she said, pointing.

Bobbie put her hand on Monee's stomach, then to the child's forehead. "You don't have a fever. Do you feel like you're going to throw up?"

"I don't know. I might."

"Then I'd better give you some medicine."

"No, Granny. It'll probably go away if I just lie here awhile."

"Well, I'll come check on you in a little bit."

Bobbie went back to the dining room. "Sorry about that. Monee isn't feeling well. We can go ahead and eat." Bobbie took the tops off the dishes and handed him a serving spoon.

"Is it serious?" he asked, serving his plate.

"I don't think so. It was rather sudden. A stomachache." When they'd served their plates, Bobbie bowed her head. Ray set his fork back down and followed suit.

After grace, Ray waited for Bobbie to take the first bite, then he plowed into his food as if he hadn't eaten in a long time. "This is even better than your gumbo."

"Thank you. I didn't have time to fix anything fancy."

"This is fancy enough for me. How did your neighbor like her room?"

"Oh, I think she really appreciated that so many of her things were there. I have you to thank for that. But she doesn't want to be there."

"Well, it's hard. Being suddenly uprooted like that. But I think you did the right thing. It's obviously not safe for her to be in that house."

"You're right. Plus, she still needs medical care. It seems like a nice place."

"By the way, I put plyboard over the window. There's no rush to replace the glass. Anybody trying to get in would go through another window. Did you make the police report?"

"Yes, I did. I had to give them your name, but I didn't know your address. I gave them your phone number too. Did they call you?"

"Not yet."

"They might not. I didn't get the impression that they were interested in the case. 'No one was hurt,' they said. I couldn't tell them anything that was missing, they said. A copy of the report would be available for me to give the insurance company, they said." Bobbie shook her head in disgust, then brightened. "Would you like seconds?"

Ray patted his stomach. "No, thank you. Everything was delicious. I usually only get home-cooked meals on Sundays if I go by Mom's. It's so late, I shouldn't eat too heavy, then go to bed. I have to watch my weight. Seems like these days, the pounds just stick. But I would take that drink now, if it's not too late."

"Sure. Let's sit in the living room."

When he was seated, she went to the cabinet in the corner. "I don't have a full bar, just the basics. I'm having a glass of wine. What about you?"

Ray thought about his years of attending officers' parties and being dragged to the Officers' Club after work. He'd spent his life around hard-drinking men. He'd have been laughed off base for prissily holding a glass of wine. Wives could drink a glass of wine, or a cute little drink with fruit in it. But this was his new life and he could try something different.

"I'll have whatever you're having."

Bobbie handed him a long-stemmed glass and sat at the other end of the couch.

"Are these your kids?" Ray asked, motioning toward the framed photo.

"Yes. Darlene and Darby."

"Looks like you had them pretty close together."

Bobbie laughed. "Yeah, real close. A couple of minutes apart. They're twins."

"Yeah, that's pretty close." Ray laughed too. "I have a couple myself. Both boys. They're two years apart, though. I needed a little time to adjust," he said with a crooked smile.

"Where are they?"

"One is a police officer in Atlanta. The other is an accountant and he lives in Kansas City. I'm so proud of both of them."

"I'm surprised they didn't go into the military, since they grew up in it."

"I'm not, really. We moved around a lot when they were growing up. I don't think either of them wanted that kind of life. What about yours? What are they doing?"

"My son is in dental school in Houston. He's graduating this semester."

"And your daughter?"

"She's here in Austin. She's, ah . . . You know, I need to check on Monee." Bobbie excused herself and walked upstairs.

When Bobbie got to Monee's door, she could hear the sounds of a video game. Monee was so engrossed in the game that she didn't hear Bobbie open the door.

"You feeling better?" Bobbie asked.

Monee jumped, then stopped the game abruptly. "Uh, yeah. My stomach doesn't hurt so much anymore." A guilty look rested on her face.

"How about some dinner now?"

Monee shook her head. "I'm real sleepy now and I just want to go to bed."

Bobbie sat on the bed and rubbed Monee's forehead. "Are you worried about Mrs. Swink?"

"Not really. Well, maybe a little."

"Well, don't worry too much. She's going to be fine."

At the door, Ray said, "I've really enjoyed the evening. I'd like to spend some more time with you—and not just to get your cooking. Could I take you out to dinner next time?"

"Sure. I'd like that," Bobbie said, leaning against the stairwell post. When it swayed under her weight, Ray caught her arm and held her steady.

Bobbie was embarrassed. "I need to get that fixed. I'm scared one day, one of us is going to lean on it and fall right over."

"It's late now, but I'll come by one day and tighten that up for you."

"Would you really? I'd sure appreciate that."

"What about Saturday? I could come by early. Then we could go look at those cabinets."

"Okay, it's a date. I mean, it's an appointment." Despite herself, Bobbie felt heat rise in her cheeks.

Ray wanted to lean over and plant a kiss on her forehead, but he was afraid she would be offended or might misconstrue his intention. In the end, he took a chance.

"You were right. It is a date." He smiled, then leaned over and planted a kiss on her forehead. "Thanks for dinner."

By Thursday, Bobbie had grown concerned about Mrs. Swink's refusal to leave her apartment. The social worker at Autumn Oaks had called Bobbie twice saying that social contact was critical to rehabilitation. Even with the cast, there was no reason Mrs. Swink couldn't take her meals in the dining room.

Bobbie had asked another teacher to take Monee home with her. Dinner was at five and now it was four-thirty. She knocked on the door to Mrs. Swink's apartment, then entered. Mrs. Swink was sitting in her rocking chair staring into space.

"Just put it on the table," she said without looking around.

"Nope. I told them not to bring your dinner today. It's time for you to get out of this room."

"That's what I want to do. I want to get out of this place. Are you taking me home?"

"Nope. I'm taking you to the dining room. Here, let me help you out of the chair."

"I don't want to. And you can't make me." Mrs. Swink gave her an obstinate glare.

Bobbie didn't back down. "Wanna bet?"

Mrs. Swink stared at her a long time, her mouth crimped in disgust. "You know, Bobbie, you can be a mean little wench when you set your mind to it."

"I'm just doing what's best for you."

"I don't want to go down there with all those old people, pushing walkers and slobbering on themselves, eating pablum."

"It's not like that."

"Okay, if it's so wonderful, I'll go if you go with me."

Bobbie looked at her watch. "Okay, deal."

At the door, Bobbie reached for the doll. "Why don't we let Mandy stay here?"

Mrs. Swink looked uncertain.

"All the new faces might frighten her. We'll go scout it out, then you can take her the next time." Mrs. Swink acquiesced and Bobbie put the doll in the chair.

Walking down the hall, Mrs. Swink leaned heavily on Bobbie's arm. They passed five other residents trudging along, pushing their walkers, and one pulling an oxygen tank behind him. In the dining hall, the social worker rushed over to greet them.

"Hi, Mrs. Swink, how nice of you to join us."

Mrs. Swink gave her a mirthless smile.

"Your assigned table is right this way. Usually there are four to a table, but there's only one at this table right now. We're expecting a couple of new people to move in this weekend, so by next week your table will be full too." Her "Let's all be happy" demeanor evoked no change in Mrs. Swink.

They followed her past several tables. Walkers, from the plain gray to fancy ones with shelves, were parked around each. Somber faces stared at them. The sounds of a hacking cough traveled from the back of the large room over the din of flatware clinking against plates.

"I'd like to have dinner too," Bobbie said. "Would that be all right? That's the only way she agreed to come."

At the table, a white-haired man sat, staring out the window.

"Mr. Rafaeli, these ladies are joining you for dinner. This is Mrs. Swink, your new tablemate, and her niece, Ms. Strickland." The old man turned briefly to look at them, nodded, then turned back to the window.

Bobbie and Mrs. Swink settled in their chairs.

"Rafaeli? Did I say that right?" Bobbie asked.

The old man didn't acknowledge her.

"Mrs. Swink is new here. Do you like it here?"

Mr. Rafaeli looked at Bobbie, twisted his mouth into a "You figure," then turned back to the window. For a moment, Bobbie thought that this might not have been such a good idea. The dining room had an oppressive air of depression. But what choice did she have?

An attendant brought bowls of soup and set them down on the table.

"Pablum," Mrs. Swink muttered under her breath.

"Pablum is *not* green," Bobbie retorted, dipping her spoon into the bowl of split-pea soup.

"Poison," Mr. Rafaeli said without turning from the window.

They both turned to look at him.

"Green is for poison. I wouldn't eat that if I were you. It's what they use to get you. Next thing you know, you'll be pushing a walker and they'll have you in diapers. Poison, I tell ya!"

"Oh, come now," Bobbie said. "It can't be poison. It just looks like . . . poison."

Mrs. Swink gave a little titter.

An attendant stopped her cart next to the table and set out three plates for them.

"This looks delicious," Bobbie said, a false tone of cheerfulness in her voice. She spread a napkin in Mrs. Swink's lap. "Do you want me to cut it for you?"

Mrs. Swink looked at the cast on her arm, then gave Bobbie a wry look.

"This doesn't taste so bad," Bobbie said.

"Mystery meat. Must be Thursday." Mr. Rafaeli hadn't turned from the window.

"What's the breakfast like?" Bobbie asked.

"A little better. The coffee's the best thing."

"Oh, that sounds good. Would either of you like a cup? I'm going to get myself one."

Both of them shook their heads, so Bobbie walked to the self-service bar across the room.

"You don't have to be so rude to me," Mrs. Swink said to Mr. Rafaeli. "I don't want to be here any more than you do. What are you staring at that's so interesting out that window?"

"That boy."

Mrs. Swink followed his gaze. "What's he doing?"

"I know one thing, he better not cut my roses. He's just supposed to edge the beds."

"What roses? I don't see any roses."

"They're on the other side of the courtyard there. You probably can't see them from here."

"I like roses. I have a whole bed of them at my house. I have a President Lincoln. That's my prize."

"Well, you can just forget about your President Lincoln. She's gonna sell your house and you'll be stuck here just like the rest of us. The only way out of this place is when the big black station wagon comes for you."

Mrs. Swink recoiled. "You're a mean, ugly man. And you're rude. And I'm not going to eat with you."

By the time Mrs. Swink had struggled out of the chair, Bobbie was walking up with the cup of coffee.

"I did what you wanted, Bobbie. Now I'm going to my room."

Sighing, Bobbie made a mental note to call the director in the morning and have Mrs. Swink moved to another table.

12

WHEN SHE got home Thursday night, Bobbie used the quiet time, while Monee prepared for bed, to sort through the pile of letters that had accumulated on the kitchen counter over the last few days. She shouldn't have let it go this long, she thought, as she idly dropped credit card offers and other solicitations in the trash can and put the bills in a pile to pay on the first of the month. One thick white envelope she knew contained a wedding invitation. The return address told her it was from Doretha's daughter. She put it aside to open later. Bobbie hated going to weddings. They only reminded her that she had been cheated out of hers. When she'd told Thomas she was pregnant, he had denied he was the father and claimed she was trying to trick him into getting married because he was the star basketball player with a good career ahead of him after college. When the twins were young, none of the men who showed interest in her had shown any interest in marriage. And now at her age, she knew she would never walk down the aisle. She'd known that for a long time.

The letter from the lawyer got her attention and she tore it open. By the time she'd finished reading it, a heavy feeling had settled in her stomach and her lips were pressed into a tight line. The return address struck her as odd. She couldn't afford a lawyer with an office on a double-digit floor in a downtown high-rise building. She wondered how Darlene could. She had been involved in several lawsuits over incidents at school, but the district had always provided the lawyer. Now she needed one to defend herself against her own child. Maybe she should try to get in touch with Darlene and work this thing out between them. But what was there to work out? She understood the pressure Darlene was under. But maybe she didn't. She'd never been faced with prison. But then, she'd never done anything to put herself in that position. When she was in high school, she'd stayed up late one night, watching a movie about a woman who went to prison. The guards were butchy and sadistic. There were fights, and a rape scene. She'd had nightmares about it for a week. And now her child was about to go to a horrible place like that.

For a hot second, Bobbie considered letting Darlene move back in her house. A hot second worth of memories was all that took. Maybe she should just let Darlene take Monee for a little while. But Bobbie knew there could be no circumstance under which she would allow Darlene to have Monee, and especially since Darlene kept that hophead, Antonio, coming around. But what if a judge ordered her to do it? She'd just go to jail. But then she wouldn't have Monee, so what would be the point? She'd take Monee and run away. But where? And wouldn't that get her in trouble? She decided she was thinking too far ahead. Maybe she should call the lawyer at the church. Maybe she could tell her what to do.

Bobbie didn't really know Mrs. Black, although over time they had spoken and nodded to each other at church. Bobbie looked at her watch. It was kind of late. But Mrs. Black's office was in her home. Maybe she should wait until tomorrow to call. But she looked back at the letter. It gave her a deadline of tomorrow. She picked up the phone.

"Geraldine Black here."

"Uh, Mrs. Black. I don't know if you remember me, but we belong to the same church and I sing in the choir. I mean, my name is Bobbie Strickland, and I have a daughter. And a granddaughter. And I'm sorry to call you so late, but I got this letter. And—"

"Ms. Strickland, why did you call me? And at this ungodly hour?"

A hundred flippant answers ran through Bobbie's mind. Finally she took a deep breath and gave the simple one: "I need help."

"What kind of help?"

Bobby wasn't liking this woman at all and decided she had made a mistake in calling her. She almost hung up, but tomorrow was on the way.

"I just figured since we belong to the same church . . . actually, I try to live my life so I don't have to know any lawyers. So now that I have this little problem, I thought because of the church you would—"

"What makes you need a lawyer in the middle of the night?"

Bobby wanted to tell this woman that nine o'clock is *not* the middle of the night, but she held her tongue. "They're trying to take my granddaughter away from me. I'm . . . scared."

"Custody? I don't handle that kind of case anymore. But there is a lawyer in my office who does. Come to the office first thing in the morning. Good night, Ms. Strickland."

Bobbie rose from her bed the next morning almost as tired as when she had gotten in it. All night long she had tossed and turned, considering how empty her life would be without Monee. No more running all over town to take her to music lessons, to gymnastics classes, to Brownie Scout meetings. What would she do with her weekends? What would she do with her evenings? Maybe she could teach the adult literacy class as she'd always planned. But now that didn't seem important at all. So many days she had resented the demands Monee made on her time, had been fretful at having too much to do. Now she regretted every moment that she'd felt that way.

And what would Monee's life be like with Darlene, living from pillar to post, being exposed to Lord knows what? The mere thought of Monee leading the kind of life that Darlene could provide made Bobbie's skin crawl—and strengthened her resolve. She smoothed the covers over the bed and walked to her closet to start her day, calling out to Monee to hurry and get ready for school.

★   ★   ★

An hour later, Bobbie had dropped Monee off at her school and driven back to the Eastside. She pulled her car to the curb in front of the big, two-story house. A small sign in the neatly trimmed lawn read BLACK & KLINE, ATTORNEYS AT LAW. The only paper that she had brought was the letter from the lawyer. She didn't know what else to bring. Birth certificate? School records? Would they be relevant? Besides, she hadn't had time to find those things. She sat in the car, girding herself.

The last time she'd hired a lawyer, not much had come of it. She had put aside her shame and hurt to force Thomas to pay child support. It just got to the point that it didn't seem fair that she and her parents had to bear the entire burden of the twins. Even though he denied the kids were his, she knew better. And he knew better too. For a while, her pride told her, "If he isn't man enough to take care of his kids, you don't even want him to." But day care was expensive, and doubly expensive for two. The lawyer had told her that if Thomas didn't agree to pay, it would be an uphill battle. That it would cost a lot of money. That the typical amount ordered for a black woman at the time was $60 a month. That piddly amount wouldn't cover half of her day-care bill, let alone food and clothing. The twins were growing so fast, and they seemed to need all new clothes at the change of every season. She always dressed them nicely, even when money was so tight that she had to shop at Goodwill. When she set the $60 against the amount the lawyer had quoted as his "estimated" fee, she could see that it would take a long time for her to get back in the black. So she paid the lawyer the consultation fee and dropped the matter. She did try to persuade Thomas to help her. And occasionally, he gave her a little money. But he always made it seem as if he was doing her a favor, rather than taking care of his responsibility. And it was never enough to really matter. Occasionally, his mother would send her a check. It was a bit more substantial. And Bobbie always wrote a nice thank-you note. Finally she gave up on Thomas. She and the kids made it just fine without him. She'd worn some panty hose with runs, pretending out loud all day long that she had just snagged them. She'd never been able to buy a brand-new car, but she *had* been able to buy the house.

Now, having to expose her life to a woman she had never met made her uneasy. But Darlene's lawyer was threatening to take her to court. And that would be very public, exposing to the whole town that she had failed with her own daughter. She could hear the tongues wagging now: "And she s'posed to be a principal. S'posed to be raising our children. Couldn't even raise her own decent." But what about Darby? He was doing so well. About to graduate from dental school. Still, that was no excuse for her failure with Darlene. She had thought and thought, and prayed and prayed. She couldn't fathom why one child would turn out just as she'd raised him to be, and the other would go so far off the path. She'd brought them both up in the church. And in fact, Darlene had shown more interest in church than Darby had. He just went along because she wanted him to, and later because of the cute girls. But Darlene had been quite active in church activities. She sang in the youth choir. She worked in the church nursery some Sundays. She had even worked in Reverend Jackson's office. Bobbie had felt particularly encouraged by that because she felt that would help keep Darlene on the straight and narrow through the turbulent teen years.

But somewhere around sixteen, Darlene had grown moody and secretive. Bobbie heard whispered phone conversations late in the night, through the door to Darlene's bedroom, which was closed all the time then. Bobbie attributed it all to normal teenage hormonal surges. Even when she'd caught Darlene sneaking in the house way past midnight a couple of times, Bobbie had tried to remember what her teenage years had been like. Of course, she'd never had the nerve to do something like that. Well, there had been that time when she'd told her parents that lie about a flat tire. Or was it running out of gas? Whatever. Her disbelieving parents had grounded her for a month. She'd tried grounding Darlene. Ha! She'd asked Reverend Jackson to counsel Darlene, thinking that a male influence was what she needed, and later he said that he had. But Darlene's behavior became increasingly unacceptable, increasingly hostile toward her. Bobbie had tried being stern. She'd tried being understanding. She'd tried being friendly. Nothing she tried had stopped Darlene's sassy mouth. Her house became a war zone. She threatened to put Darlene out, but by then she was a principal, and she knew the law of parental responsibility. Some days, Bobbie thought she would lose her mind. During the day, she counseled parents to be understanding with their kids. At night she had the screaming meemies with her own. Then Darlene had gotten pregnant, and Bobbie's world had come crashing down. All her hopes and dreams had been shattered.

Is that why she was here in the lawyer's office now? she wondered. Was it the part of her that was still hurt and angry at Darlene? Was it the part of her that felt used and abused because her life had been put off track by Darlene's irresponsibility? Was it that part that said, After I gave up my young years for you, you've deprived me of the peace I'm entitled to at this time in my life? In the end, she knew it wasn't because Darlene had made her a statistic—teenage mother of a teenage mother. This wasn't about Darlene at all. It was about Monee. Bobbie grabbed her purse and marched determined toward the door.

A small, neatly printed sign read KNOCK, THEN ENTER, so she did. Bobbie would have described the woman who greeted her as handsome. About her age. Bobbie could tell the plain linen dress she wore didn't fit in Bobbie's own budget. Everything about the woman, down to the simple wedding band with ten diamonds, said expensive—except her smile.

"Good morning. I'm Vivian Kline. You must be Mrs. Strickland?"

Bobbie nodded and corrected her. "*Ms.* Strickland."

"Mrs. Black told me to expect you. Would you come into my office?" she asked, leading the way. "You look like you could use a cup of coffee."

"No, thank you," Bobbie answered, then reconsidered. "Yes. I'd like a cup." Bobbie stood and watched as Vivian prepared two cups of coffee. The high-ceilinged office was homey and welcoming. A degree from UT Law School and the state bar license in matching frames of simple teak hung on the wall behind a plain desk.

"Let's sit over here," Vivian said, motioning to the sofa. When they were settled, Vivian said, "I understand you have a custody problem. Someone is trying to take your child?"

"My grandchild."

"Why don't you tell me about it."

"Let's see, where do I start? My granddaughter is nine years old. I have had her most of her life because my daughter is . . . un . . . a . . . irresponsible. Monee was born out of wedlock when Darlene—that's my daughter—was in high school."

Bobbie almost added, "Just like me." But she had at least been nineteen. In the end, she decided it wasn't important.

"Anyway, she was in and out of my house for the first couple of years after the baby was born. But even then, I was mostly responsible for Monee's care. I tried to give them both stability. Even though Darlene was a teenager, she was still a child. I guess you have teenagers, so you know what I mean."

"No. My girls are two and three." When she saw Bobbie's raised eyebrow, Vivian added with a soft chuckle, "I got a late start. But that's a long story. Anyway, where were we?"

"Well, Darlene thought that since she had a baby, she was grown and could just do as she pleased. But you know the average house can't tolerate but about one grown woman, and I am the grown woman in my house. Anyway, we'd have a big blowout and she'd leave for a while, then come back dragging that baby, sick and runny-nosed. Finally, one time she left the baby with me and didn't come back for months. And frankly, I was glad. I nursed that baby back to health and we settled into a fairly normal life, and Darlene got used to being free. So it's been that way ever since. I'm sorry. I'm sort of babbling, huh?"

"That's all right. Take your time. This is good background information."

"Well, all these years went by. I want you to understand that Darlene isn't a bad person. I mean, she wasn't raised to be a bad person. She got involved with the wrong crowd. Drugs and all. It got to the point I had to change the locks on my door and I couldn't even let my own child in my house. Every time she'd leave, something would turn up missing. She even took the baby's Christmas presents once. Finally, she got in trouble with the law. She's on probation, but she hasn't been doing what she's supposed to. And she says that now the judge is trying to send her to prison. But she'll let her stay out because she has a child. But she doesn't really have a child. Monee is my child. I'm the one who's raised her."

"Can she take care of the child?"

Bobbie rolled her eyes, crimped her lips, and blew out a choppy, angry breath. "She can't take care of her damn self. Doesn't have a job. She just moved into a center for abused women, for God's sake. And she wants to take Monee to live there. And this silly-assed—excuse me, I mean, her caseworker is supporting her in that."

"Have you received any orders from the judge?"

Bobbie shook her head.

"Have you and Darlene ever been to court over this?"

Bobbie shook her head again.

"Well, under these circumstances, I don't think you have anything to worry about. It doesn't sound to me like your daughter can take care of Mo-nee—did I say her name right? If she isn't working and doesn't have any money, she won't have access to the courts. That's just a fact. A sad fact. But a fact just the same. Now, the way I see it, you have two choices. You can just keep on doing what you've been doing and not worry about this, or—"

"But Darlene says she can just take Monee because she's

her mother. What if she just takes her? What can I do? Can I call the police?"

Vivian's brow wrinkled. "Well, the police probably can't help you under these circumstances. They would probably say there's nothing they can do. And they would be right. The natural parent's right is superior."

"But Monee would be traumatized."

Vivian nodded. "You're probably right. If you want to be on the safe side, you can file in court to be appointed as managing conservator of the child. It's almost certain that you'll be appointed—"

"Good. How much would that cost?"

"Well, that depends on how much of a fight your daughter puts up. And once you invoke the jurisdiction of the court, invite them into your business, you can't get them out until the child is eighteen. So you'd have yearly legal expenses. You need to know that judges are charged to do what they can to strengthen the parent-child bond. As part of that proceeding your daughter will probably be given specified rights to visitation that you will be required to honor. Can you live with that?"

Bobbie's immediate answer was no.

"And there will be a home study. The judge will appoint an ad litem to represent the child, probably someone in the Domestic Relations office. That person will investigate both your circumstances and your daughter's. Then they'll make a report to the court. And in your daughter's situation, the court will appoint a lawyer for her."

"That won't be necessary." Bobbie reached in her purse, took the envelope out, and handed it to Vivian. "She already has a lawyer."

Vivian's whole countenance stiffened when she saw the return address.

"I'm sorry, Ms. Strickland. You'll have to consult a different lawyer. I can't handle this case," she said, handing the letter back to Bobbie.

"Why?" Bobbie asked, trying to keep the alarm she felt from her voice. "You're the only lawyer I know. I've already taken off half a day from my job. And I don't have time to find another lawyer. This letter says Darlene is going to go to Monee's school today and take her." Bobbie heard the desperation in her voice. She could tell that Vivian heard it too.

"Well, you can get an injunction to stop her from doing that until a judge can get both sides in court," Vivian said in a soothing tone, as though that wouldn't be a problem. But her brow was furrowed, and she twisted the wedding band on her finger around and around as if she knew it would be.

"So, how do I do that?" Bobbie asked.

Vivian looked at her watch and sighed. "I'm afraid you'd have to have a lawyer. Somebody who knows the ropes, someone who knows how to get this done on an emergency basis."

"Don't you know how to do that?"

"I'm sorry. I really am. I do know how, but I have a personal relationship that poses a conflict."

"What? You know my daughter?" Bobbie's voice rose in surprise and she looked at Vivian with suspicion.

"No, not your daughter. Her lawyer."

"So? I imagine you know most of the lawyers in town."

"Mr. Carlson is my ex-husband."

"So what? Are you scared of him or something? Still love him?"

"No, of course not." Vivian threw her chin up at the challenge.

"Then what's your problem? I'm the one with the problem."

Vivian didn't answer right away. Bobbie could tell from the look on her face that Vivian was trying to decide how straight she could be with Bobbie.

"I guess I'm afraid of you," Vivian finally answered. "See, right now, you're the one with the problem. If I sign on to this case, it becomes my problem. That's what we lawyers are paid to do—worry about other people's problems. Then, if it doesn't turn out the way you want, you could accuse me of something . . . improper."

"Listen, Mrs. Kline, I'm just trying to protect my grandbaby. She's just a little girl. While you're sitting around pondering whether you really still love your ex-husband or not, or whether I will sue you, a little girl could be taken from a safe and clean home to a drug den—or something worse. What if it was one of your little girls? I need your help."

13

THE BENCH she sat on was so hard it hurt her behind, and the secretary occasionally eyed her as if to say, "Are you still here?" Bobbie looked at her watch, then back at the door to the judge's office. Vivian had been in there a long time. Every now and then, she would hear muffled laughter. How could they be in there having such a good time when she was sitting here picking at her cuticles until one of them bled?

As soon as Vivian had agreed to represent her, Bobbie had called Monee's school and talked with the principal. She knew him well, not only from her numerous trips to the school, but also from the quarterly Circle of Principals meetings. He had assured her that he would call her if anyone came to get Monee and that he would not allow anyone to take her without a court order. What that said to Bobbie was that she had to get there with her own court order first. Even though she hadn't heard it ring, she took her cell phone out of her purse and looked at the caller ID listing just to make sure he hadn't tried to call.

She impatiently tapped her foot on the marble floor, thinking of how long her morning had been, and all the work that awaited her at school. The secretary's annoyed look made Bobbie still her foot. Earlier, she'd sat next to Vivian, giving her the information to fill in blanks on her computer. Then she'd waited what seemed like an interminable time while the pages came out of the printer. If she'd had the computer program, she could have prepared those papers herself. But this was the part she couldn't do. Vivian had effortlessly run the traps that got the papers filed and got them into the judge's private chambers.

The door opened and they walked out, Vivian shaking the judge's hand. Bobbie gathered up her purse and stood to greet him, but he walked back into his office and closed the door.

"Come on. One more trip by the clerk's office to get the order filed and prepared for the process server."

"How long is that going to take?"

"Not long. I have a server standing by to deliver the order to Darlene and her lawyer. Then he can take a copy to Monee's school."

"Can I take it to the school? I'm going by there anyway."

"That'll be fine. We have a hearing set for next week. In the meantime, I want you to come by the office Monday so we can talk in more detail about the facts of the case. And I want you to be thinking about what kind of visitation would be okay with you."

★   ★   ★

That afternoon, Bobbie sat at her desk prioritizing the stack of telephone messages Olga had given her, and tried not to think about the morning's events. She kept the one from Scott Douglas, the school district's lawyer, on top, one from the Autumn Oaks director next, then the Police Department Tele-report Section, Darlene's caseworker, then Ms. Thompson. She put the one from Bill Gibson on the bottom. To hell with Bill.

"Mr. Douglas, this is Bobbie Strickland, principal at Barbara Jordan Elementary. I'm returning your call."

Scott Douglas told her what she had known from the moment she'd seen his name on the pink message slip that DeShawn's mother had made good on her threat. Ms. Thompson's lawyer had sent a notice of intent to file a lawsuit against the school district, against Bill Gibson—and against Bobbie. Yes, she could come to his office next week and bring all the documents relating to the incident. Yes, she understood that she should make no comment to the media or anyone else. Yes, she understood she could not institute proceedings to remove DeShawn from school. No, she didn't have her own lawyer.

From the director at Autumn Oaks, she got a list of items Mrs. Swink needed from her house and from the grocery store. And had she made a decision about signing the year's lease? No, they wouldn't be able to move Mrs. Swink to another table in the dining room at this time.

The Police Department Tele-report Section wanted to verify the address of the incident. Verify the address? Bobbie felt like slamming the phone down. They should have been halfway through the investigation by now—and they weren't even sure of the address.

Bobbie was relieved that Darlene's caseworker was in a group session when she called, so she left a message that she'd returned her call and quickly hung up. She paused at the message from Ms. Thompson. It went against her grain not to return a phone call, even one she expected to be unpleasant. But if she called her, all she could say is that she couldn't talk to her now that lawyers were involved. There was no telling how Ms. Thompson would take her not returning the call. In the end, she put the message in the file she planned to take to Douglas. The last person on earth she wanted to talk to was Bill Gibson. But she might as well get it over with.

"Bill, did you need something?"

"I sure do. Have you talked to the lawyer? I need your support on this thing, Bobbie. It's your job to support the staff. We've got to stick together. We've got to be on the same page. Tell the same story."

Even in his smooth-talking tone, fear could be heard in Bobbie's voice. The little weasel thought he could do her job. Now at the first sign of real trouble, he was running to her to fix it.

"Number one, I don't need you to tell me what my job is. Number two, there's no 'story' here, only the truth." Bobbie wanted to add, "I'm going to support you in the same way you've been supporting me," but instead she dropped the phone back on the receiver.

Later, Bobbie picked Monee up and drove straight to Autumn Oaks. They would only have a few minutes to visit before Monee's gymnastics lesson. Dinner would be over, so she expected to find Mrs. Swink in her room. When she didn't come to the door in response to her knock, Bobbie used the extra key the director had given her to let them in. Mrs. Swink wasn't there.

"Mandy is gone too, Granny," Monee said from the bedroom. "These are pretty flowers."

Distracted, Bobbie looked at her watch. The dining hall would be closed. Someone had posted the monthly activity calendar on the wall over the dinette table. She looked for today's date and saw that the only activities at this time were a prayer service and a domino tournament. For a moment, Bobbie's spirit was uplifted. She had never known Mrs. Swink to play dominoes, so maybe she had gone to the prayer service. That was a good sign. She and Monee walked down the hall and around the corner to the other wing, looking for the chapel. Three people were in the chapel other than the speaker. But not Mrs. Swink. They stopped back at the office, but the woman on duty didn't know where Mrs. Swink was. Alarm ran through Bobbie. Maybe she had tried to go home. But how could she do that? A taxi? Maybe she had wandered off and was walking the streets with a cast on one arm and the doll tucked under the other—advertising herself as easy prey. Bobbie didn't know what to do.

"Do you have an intercom system?" she asked the woman.

"Yes, but we only use it for emergencies. We don't want to alarm the residents."

"But this is an emergency."

"Not really. There's any number of places in the building that she could be. We have three or four sitting areas on each floor. Then the crafts room. The washroom. Why don't you look around. She's probably just visiting her friends. Nothing to worry about."

"She doesn't have any friends here." Bobbie looked at her watch again and started rearranging her schedule. Monee would just have to miss gymnastics. "Come on, Monee, let's go look for her."

When they turned the corner to the second wing, they saw Mrs. Swink walking toward them with the Mandy doll in the crook of her arm. Monee ran to her and threw her arms around her waist. Bobbie was glad she had brought Monee. The smile on Mrs. Swink's face relieved her. As they walked at Mrs. Swink's pace to her room, Bobbie checked her watch again. They could have a short visit, and Monee could still make her lesson. Bobbie would have to speed—and pray that she didn't get a ticket.

"Where've you been? We've been looking all over for you," Bobbie said.

"I was just around," Mrs. Swink answered without looking at her.

"Around where?"

"We were . . . I thought maybe Zeke would come looking for us. I tried to find the lobby after dinner. I got a little lost." Mrs. Swink looked sheepish.

"Well, I'm glad you found your way back." A frown played on Bobbie's forehead. Tomorrow she would call the doctor about Mrs. Swink's continued confusion.

"That Italian fellow showed me."

Bobbie looked at her quizzically.

"You remember that old Italian man from dinner?"

"Oh, yes. The rude one? I'm trying to get you moved from his table."

Mrs. Swink cut her eyes at Bobbie. "He's not so bad. Just lonesome." Mrs. Swink looked at the doll and smiled. "He said Mandy is the prettiest little girl he's ever seen. He and his wife didn't have girls, you know."

"This is your door here." Bobbie pushed the door open and they went in. "You took Mandy to dinner?"

"She didn't want to stay here by herself, Bobbie."

Bobbie heard the balkiness in her voice and decided not to argue. She would certainly speak to the doctor about it, though.

"We've got to run. I'll check on you tomorrow."

"You haven't brought my Bible."

"Oh, shoot. I forgot. I'm sorry. Why can't you read the one here?"

"I need it for something." Mrs. Swink's brow wrinkled and her eyes squinted in thought. "I just can't . . . just bring it, okay?"

Bobbie had to ask the question that had been nagging at her. She turned to Monee. "Honey, you head on down to the lobby. I'll be there in a minute."

Monee gave Mrs. Swink a big hug and closed the door behind her.

"Mrs. Swink, where is your ruby ring?"

Mrs. Swink spread her hand out in front of her and looked surprised that it wasn't on her finger. She looked up at Bobbie with a blank expression.

"Do you remember the last time you saw it?"

Mrs. Swink twisted her mouth, trying to remember.

"Do you remember giving it to Darlene?" Bobbie held her breath.

"Did she say I gave it to her?" When Bobbie didn't

answer, Mrs. Swink searched her face for a clue, then looked off. "Oh, yes. I remember now. I gave it to Darlene. She's such a sweet girl."

"When?" Bobbie couldn't hide the skepticism in her voice.

Mrs. Swink still wouldn't look at her. "Oh, it wasn't too long ago. One day, she came by." She sneaked a peek at Bobbie and saw that she was unconvinced, so she began adding details. "I remember. We had a cup of tea. And she read the newspaper to me. Yeah, that was the day. I remember because I told her she was looking real thin."

"Why would you give Darlene your ring? I thought it meant so much to you. That Zeke had given it to you."

Mrs. Swink crooked her head. "Well, she looked so down in the dumps. And she gave me . . . something." She squinted her eyes again, trying to force the memory to come. "I can't remember. But it seemed real important to her. So I gave her the ring."

Bobbie wasn't sure whether to believe her or not. "Do you want me to get the ring back for you?"

"No. Darlene's a good girl, Bobbie. She'll take care of my ring. I know you haven't gotten over her having the baby and all. But that doesn't make her a bad girl. And just look at the joy that child has brought to your life."

"Speaking of Monee, I'd better go. I'll check on you tomorrow."

14

BOBBIE PICKED up the phone, but the line was dead. Thinking the racket she was hearing must be her alarm clock, she reached over and hit the snooze button, even though she didn't think she'd set the alarm last night. She'd had the week from hell and had fully intended to sleep in this morning. She had thought that her schedule was full before, but now having to squeeze in a visit to Mrs. Swink every day on top of everything else had seemingly compressed hours into minutes. She'd fallen in bed each night exhausted. She'd even missed choir rehearsal Thursday night. She'd planned to sleep until she woke up this morning, so she knew she hadn't set the alarm. But it was ringing again. Out of one drowsy eye, she could see the clock read six-thirty.

Bobbie sat bolt upright in the bed. She jumped out of the bed, grabbed her robe, then started down the stairs. Through the peephole, she could see that it was Ray. A toolbox sat on the porch by his foot. She cracked the door an eye's width.

"Good morning. Jesus, you're up early."

"I told you I'd come by early to fix the post."

"Yeah, but you didn't say the middle of the night."

Ray laughed. "I do my best work in the morning. Are you gonna open the door?"

"Well, not now. I'm not even up."

"Well, let me in. Then you can go back to bed. I don't need your help with this little project."

"But I'm not dressed."

"Okay, how about you leave the door unlocked, I'll give you a minute or two to go back to bed, then I'll let myself in and get to work."

Bobbie looked around the living room, then said, "Give me five minutes." She pushed the door closed, made a whirlwind tour of the living room, grabbing up Monee's dolls and books. She stuffed them all in the closet at the foot of the stairs, then hurried to her room. She didn't even think about getting back in the bed. She spread the covers on the bed before pulling on a pair of jeans and a T-shirt. In the bathroom, she brushed her teeth and made her face and hair as presentable as she could on short notice. The image reflected back to her from the mirror looked dowdy. She knotted the tail of the T-shirt at her waist, then put on a hint of lipstick. Better.

When she stepped into the hall, she had a clear view of him at the bottom of the stairs. He was squatting down, reaching into the open toolbox. He looked up at that moment and a little smile formed on his lips.

"Can a hardworking fella get a cup of coffee around this joint?"

"It'll cost you a quarter," she said, walking down the

stairs. When she got to the bottom, he leaned over to let her pass. "I guess next you'll want breakfast."

Shortly, Bobbie returned with two steaming cups. She sat on the second step from the bottom and set his cup within his reach. "You owe me a quarter."

He laughed. "I'm almost done here. I've shimmed this base and glued it. I'll need to leave these clamps on it for at least twenty-four hours. Don't put any pressure on it." He took a length of blue nylon cord and tied it around the top of the post. "This'll remind you." Ray picked up the cup and took a sip. "Ooh, that's good." He set the cup back on the stair, gathered up his tools, and put them back in the tool-box.

"You wanna go on the porch and finish your coffee?" Bobbie asked.

"Sure."

Minutes later, Bobbie and Ray sat on the swing, Bobbie pushing her foot against the porch floor and starting the swing in a gentle motion. "How did you learn how to fix things?"

"My dad. He could fix just about anything. From as far back as I can remember, I was always in the garage with him, handing him tools, eventually working on projects of my own."

As he talked, they watched Bobbie's neighbors as they came out to get their morning newspapers. Bobbie gave him a report on each one.

"I love this time of morning," he said. "And I love swinging in your swing. Maybe you'll let me do it again some-time."

"Another cup of coffee?"

"Refills are free, right?"

She smiled, took his cup, and went inside. When she returned, she carried a tray with their two cups and two plates.

"My grits-and-eggs casserole," she announced, handing him a plate, fork, and napkin. She set the tray between them on the swing.

"Are you magic, or what? This is delicious. Did Mr. Strickland die, or was he stupid enough to let you get away?"

Bobbie didn't really know how to answer the question. Well, she knew how, she just didn't want to. She didn't want to tell him that Mr. Strickland was her daddy, and that all the rest had let her get away. There was no smooth way for her to change the subject, but she was saved when she saw Monee through the screen at the front door.

"Good morning, Monee," she said. "Come on out."

Monee slowly opened the screen and made her way over to the swing. She climbed up in the swing next to Bobbie on the side opposite Ray. She laid her head against Bobbie's shoulder as though she intended to resume her slumber. Bobbie smoothed Monee's hair and pulled her pink night-gown down to cover her legs.

"I know you must have left your manners upstairs." When Monee didn't respond to her prompt, Bobbie said, "Aren't you going to speak to Mr. Caldwell?"

Monee peeked around Bobbie, gave Ray a look of half suspicion, half resentment, and finally said, "Morning." She picked up Bobbie's fork and began to finish off the square of casserole.

"I guess if I'm going to have some breakfast, I'll have to

get another plate," Bobbie said, pulling teasingly at Monee's braid.

As soon as Bobbie was in the house, Monee turned to Ray. "You didn't tell her, did you?"

"About what? The mess you made in my truck?"

"That too."

Ray remembered about the secret. He'd thought about it before, but he didn't know how to bring up the subject to Bobbie. Or whether he should.

"Not yet. But I think *you* should" was the answer he gave Monee.

"I'm not gonna like you if you tell," Monee said with a pout on her lips.

Ray pondered that. Since the divorce, he hadn't dated a woman with young children. A couple of women whom he'd taken out had had teenagers, and one had a grown son still living at home. They had mostly ignored him, but he found it hard to ignore the disrespect they showed their moms in their speech and their mannerisms. Despite how he felt about Loretta, even now, he'd break either of his boys' necks if they treated her that way. In the end, the truth was he hadn't liked the women enough to struggle with the kids. But he thought he might just like this woman enough.

"I brought you a glass of milk, Monee," Bobbie said from the doorway. "Your piano teacher just called and canceled your lesson for today."

Monee's face lit up. "Good. We can do something fun today."

"Actually, Mr. Caldwell is going to take us to look at some cabinets."

"That doesn't sound like fun, Granny."

"We'll just make it fun, Monee. Hand me that plate, then go put on some clothes."

Monee jumped down from the swing. The sudden movement jostled Ray's cup so that he had to hold it away from him to keep it from spilling on his pants.

"Excuse me, Mr. Caldwell." Monee's countenance was so sweet and apologetic that both Bobbie and Ray softened the tight looks on their faces.

"Would you walk with me down to Mrs. Swink's house? She's been on me to bring her Bible to her. Frankly, I've been a little nervous about going down there by myself."

"Sure." Ray liked the role of protector.

They walked down the street and entered the house. Although neither of them really expected to encounter danger on a brightly lit Saturday morning, Ray went in first. Bobbie retrieved the big, gold-edged Bible from the shelf. It was clearly old, but not tattered. It had a strap around it that slipped into a lock. Bobbie pressed the little button to release the strap, but it was locked.

"This won't do her much good without the key. I wonder where it is."

She made a cursory check of the drawers in the desk next to the shelf. "Never mind. I'll ask her where the key is when I take her the Bible. Let's get out of here. Monee's probably dressed by now."

On the short walk back, Bobbie spotted the familiar Lexus driving toward them. She felt a momentary twinge of guilt. Here she was walking down the street with a man— and at nearly the crack of dawn. She wondered how that looked to the pastor. What could she say to explain it?

"I wonder what Reverend Jackson's doing over this way this time of morning. I don't know of any members who live on this street."

"Maybe he's looking to expand the flock," Ray said with a chuckle.

When the car was near enough, Bobbie knew he would recognize her, so she waved—just to make sure it didn't look as if she were hiding something, or ignoring him. The car stopped next to them and the dark-tinted window rolled down.

"Morning, Sister Strickland."

"Brother Harris, what brings you over this way?"

"Reverend Jackson asked me to have his car washed."

"I see. But there aren't any car washes near here."

"Uh, one of the young men I recruited in . . . I mean converted, was recently released. His mama lives somewhere around here. I thought I'd spend a little time with him. Make sure his mind is stayed on Jesus."

"Well, don't let me hold you up. Good to see you."

"Brother Caldwell, we sure want you to join us in this important work."

Ray just nodded and smiled. He couldn't keep his eye off the earring.

"Well, I'll be in touch." With that, the window went up, and Brother Harris drove away.

At the Home Center, Bobbie was impressed with the array of cabinets available. After walking the section three times, she showed Ray the style she liked best.

"How much would these cost?"

He pulled the paper from his pocket with the rough diagram he'd drawn, did some quick calculations, then wrote a figure on it.

"For the size of your kitchen, I figure about fifteen hundred dollars," he said, showing her the paper.

Bobbie looked at the figure and immediately thought she couldn't afford it. Then she looked back at the display and thought how nice those cabinets would look in her kitchen. Then she thought about how much time she spent in her kitchen. Then she thought about the loan she could take at the Teachers' Credit Union. She didn't have a lot of money, but she did have good credit.

"And it'll take six weeks for them to be delivered. I could build you some better-quality cabinets than these in less than six weeks."

"How much would that cost?" she asked.

"The materials would cost about the same as this."

"And the labor?"

"Well, we could work something out on that."

"Something like what?" Bobbie's antennae shot up.

Ray saw it. "I didn't mean that like you took it. Just relax. Tell you what, later I'll sit down and put pencil to paper. I'll give you an exact figure. Then we'll work it out however you're comfortable."

Bobbie felt Monee tugging at her sleeve.

"Buy me this, Granny."

"What is that?"

"It's a box. It's pretty."

It didn't look pretty to Bobbie. It was just a plain wooden box. When she took it from Monee, it felt rough in her hand. She struggled the top off it, then had trouble getting it back on. She handed it back to Monee and picked a little splinter out of her finger.

"What would you do with this? How much is it?" Bobbie asked.

"I don't know. It's pretty."

"Let me see that." Ray turned the box around in his hand. "Shoddy workmanship. Not even worth twenty bucks."

"It's only nineteen ninety-five," Bobbie said, taking the box from him.

Ray shrugged his shoulders. "It's up to you."

Bobbie thought about it a minute. "Put this back, Monee. We'll find you a better one."

Monee looked disappointed but didn't argue. As she walked off, she rolled her eyes at Ray.

He stared at the photo. She looked so young. It was a shame. But that was all in the past. What he had to do now was find the negatives. Then the job would be completed. He felt a twinge of remorse over beating the old lady. But she'd asked for it, hitting him with that cane. If she'd just done what he'd said, it wouldn't have happened. It was her fault. All she'd had to do was tell him, lie still and tell him where the stuff was. It could have been so simple. Now he'd have to go back.

He'd watched the house. He knew the old lady wasn't there because the same lamp had come on and off at regular intervals. It wasn't a big house. What he was looking for shouldn't be that hard to find, since he'd have the house to himself the next time.

15

ON THURSDAY, the hallway outside the courtroom was crowded and the air charged with tension. The family courts were on this floor. Warring husbands and wives glared at each other across the expanse of the marble floor. Little children pulled at their mothers' arms, trying to understand what was happening. One woman sat alone on a hard bench, quietly crying into her hands. A shoving match broke out but was quickly quelled by the security guard, who, with a stern warning, motioned the parties and their respective lawyers to separate corners.

Sitting next to Vivian on the hard bench, Bobbie was nervous. She was embarrassed. She hoped she didn't see anyone who knew her. She was scared and had an urge to reach for Vivian's hand, just to get a sense of security. But she didn't. She was accustomed to relying on herself. This time was no different.

Vivian pointed out Walter Carlson when the elevator door opened: "That's Darlene's lawyer."

"Your ex-husband?"

Vivian nodded. Bobbie recognized him from seeing his picture in the newspaper.

"You have good taste."

"Not really," Vivian said with a wry twist of her lips.

Bobbie saw something in Vivian's eyes that she couldn't quite put a name to. She hoped that Vivian had no love for this man, and that she wouldn't sell her down the river for him. For an instant, she thought that she might have made a mistake to insist that Vivian represent her. But at the time, it seemed like her only option.

Darlene's lawyer caught sight of them and strode in their direction as though he owned the place. Vivian immediately stood. After an awkward moment of indecision, Bobbie stood too.

"You're looking good, Vivian," he said when he reached them. "You look like a real lawyer."

"Good morning, Walter," she answered flatly. "This is my client, Ms. Strickland."

"A pleasure," Walter said to Bobbie, and shook the wooden hand that she held out to him. He turned back to Vivian. "Did you convey our offer to your client?"

"We've discussed it, in general," Vivian said noncommittally. In their meeting on Monday, Bobbie had been so adamant about keeping Monee that Vivian hadn't seen any point in going into the particulars of Walter's proposal to give custody to Darlene.

"I've drawn up the papers," Walter said. "They're just temporary orders. Of course, I've included a suitable transition period." He reached into his Moroccan-leather case and took out a folder. "The three of us can just all sign them right now—I'm authorized to sign on behalf of my client—and we won't have to wait around here all day to get a hearing. Look at this crowd." He glanced around to make his point.

"We'll discuss it," Vivian said, taking the folder from him. "But if I were you, I'd clear my calendar for the day."

"Now, Vivian, come on. You know this case is pro bono for me, and I won't make one red cent out of it. Not that I mind," he quickly added. "We can get this wrapped up and work out the details later."

"We'll discuss it," she said firmly.

"Well, be sure and tell Ms. Stickland what it's going to cost her for you to be in this courthouse all day." He turned and looked at Bobbie to make sure she'd heard him, then back at Vivian.

"The financial arrangements between my client and me are none of your business, Walter."

"Hmm, touchy, aren't we?" A little smile turned one corner of his mouth.

"Is your client here?" Vivian asked.

He didn't answer for a long minute. "She'll be here if she needs to be. I'll give you a few minutes to look over the order." He turned and walked toward the courtroom.

Vivian sucked her teeth impatiently, then scanned the first page, with Bobbie peeking over her shoulder. A hush in the hallway drew Vivian's attention. She looked at her watch.

"It's a minute before docket call. You can stay here and read this, but I don't think it's what you want. Looks like we're going to trial. I'll just go make our announcement and see where we stand in the lineup. I'll be back in a few minutes."

After Vivian left, Bobbie sat down and returned to reading the paper. She grew angrier with each sentence. These papers gave custody to Darlene. She and Vivian hadn't discussed that at all. She'd told Vivian that she didn't want Darlene to have any unsupervised visitation with Monee. And she didn't want Darlene in her house. Vivian had tried to persuade her to adopt a more reasonable position. She thought the judge would be interested in strengthening the parent-child relationship. Bobbie had had to admit that Darlene had never done anything to physically harm Monee. And she'd admitted that she didn't believe Darlene would. Still, that she'd left Monee with Bobbie all these years, that Bobbie had had to put her life on hold, showed that Darlene didn't deserve to have Monee. Vivian had said all she could to persuade Bobbie to agree to something. Bobbie refused to believe that a judge would change the arrangement that had evolved over the years between her and Darlene. She thought stability for Monee should be paramount. Vivian had sighed in resignation, "I'll do what I can."

The door to the courtroom opened and Vivian and Walter walked through together. They paused just outside the door and talked. Bobbie thought they stood closer together than adversaries would. They were a handsome couple. Bobbie wondered what had happened to their marriage. She saw Walter reach for Vivian's hand, and the earnest look on his face. Vivian glanced Bobbie's way, then pulled her hand back. She walked to where Bobbie sat and Walter got on the elevator.

"We're number six," Vivian said. "Looks like it's going to be a long day. I think a couple of the cases ahead of us may settle. Still, it looks like we won't be reached until close to lunchtime. Maybe after. I gave the bailiff my cell phone number. He'll call when we get close. Let's go to the coffee shop."

The call came at 10:51. Vivian and Bobbie hurried to the fifth floor and waited outside the courtroom door. When the elevator door opened and she saw Darlene, Bobbie's jaw dropped. Darlene wore a navy suit that was clean and pressed. Her hair was straightened and pulled back in a bun. She looked like a responsible adult. She looked like someone Bobbie would have trusted with a child. She looked like a daughter Bobbie would have been proud of. Bobbie felt as if someone were playing a trick on her. Darlene looked at her uncertainly, then slowly walked over.

"Hi, Mama."

"Hi yourself, Darlene."

Darlene looked as if she didn't know what to say next. Bobbie felt a rush of maternal feelings. She felt like gathering her child up in her arms and smoothing away the worry that showed on her face. She felt like slapping the fool out of her. Why did it have to be this way? Why did they have to have these strangers in their business?

The courtroom was old and smelled of mold. Next to Bobbie at the counsel table, Vivian organized books and stacks of papers. Across the aisle from Vivian at the other table,

Walter sat calmly. There was nothing on his table but a Montblanc pen. Next to him, Darlene kept looking over her shoulder.

The judge whisked in and sat at the bench before any of them could get to their feet.

"Case number 142595. In the matter of Monika Tanisha Strictland. Counsel, announce your appearance."

When the formalities had been dispensed with, the judge looked at Vivian. She stood.

"Your Honor, my client, Barbara Strickland, is request-ing to be appointed temporary managing conservator of the nine-year old child. The child has been in her care and cus-tody nearly since birth. We expect to show that the mother of the child is in no position to care for the child at this time and that it would be in the best interest of the child to con-tinue to live with her grandmother in the only home she's ever known."

Vivian called Bobbie to the stand, asked her to identify herself by name, address, and occupation. She asked Bobbie a series of questions that laid out the facts to support her request for custody.

Then it was Walter's turn to cross-examine. He absently tapped the pen on the table five or six times before he spoke.

"Ms. Strickland, are you married?"

"No."

"Have you ever been married?"

Bobbie lowered her eyes. "No," she said in a quiet voice.

"What kind of social life do you have?"

"I beg your pardon?"

"What do you do for fun?"

Bobbie thought about that for a long time. She supposed

she must have had some fun sometime. She just couldn't think of any right offhand. What if the judge thought it was important that a young girl live in a fun-filled environment, taking regular trips to Disneyland? She wondered if their church trip to Sea World in San Antonio counted. She could feel the tension lines in her forehead, the tightness around her mouth. If she looked the way she felt, the judge probably thought of her as stern and harsh. She tried to relax her face. She knew she was taking too long to answer the question. Maybe that told the answer. "I hadn't thought about it" was wrong. "I consider education more important" sounded pretentious and defensive.

"I belong to the choir." That sounded weak, even to her. And it wasn't that the choir was fun. It gave her a sense of purpose. Gave her a sense of belonging. It gave her release. But fun?

"What about boyfriends?"

Bobbie frowned. She didn't know exactly how to answer that either. She couldn't rightly say that Ray was her boyfriend. She wanted him to be something, other than just her carpenter. But right now he was just her carpenter.

"A woman my age doesn't have boyfriends, Mr. Carlson." Bobbie heard the righteous indignation. She wished she hadn't said it.

"What *does* a woman your age have, Ms. Strickland?"

"Objection. Argumentative," Vivian said.

"Withdraw the question. I would think that an attractive woman like you would have a, ah, what shall we say, a man friend."

Bobbie stared at him. She wanted to say, "That's none of your damned business." But he hadn't asked a question and she didn't answer one. Vivian had told her to be careful about that.

"Did you bring the child to court today?"

"No."

"Why not?"

"Because it's a school day and I thought it was more important that Monee go to school."

"Are you sure it wasn't because you didn't want the judge to talk to the child herself? Aren't you afraid that the child will say that she loves her mother and wants to be with her mother?"

"No, I'm not afraid about that. Monee loves her mother. She *should* love her mother."

Bobbie didn't answer his other question. This was the first time she'd thought about what Monee would want. She hadn't asked her. And Monee's opinion didn't count anyway. She was just a child. What would she know about the dangers involved in her mother's lifestyle? What kind of person would she become without the advantages that Bobbie could provide? Would all of Bobbie's sacrifice come to naught? Bobbie knew the answers to those questions. But there was one that she didn't know the answer to.

Would Monee tell the judge that she wanted to live with her mother?

16

DARLENE LOOKED like a little girl on the witness stand. Bobbie could see the precious little girl that Darlene had been, just beneath the grown-up attire. It almost brought tears to her eyes. This was the part she knew would be hard for her to sit through. To have a stranger attack her child would be like having a knife plunged in her heart. She'd told Vivian all of the things that would make Darlene look bad in the eyes of the judge, including about Antonio. Now she almost wished she hadn't. She focused her attention on the question Vivian was asking.

"Where do you live?"

"Ma'am, I live at a facility called the House of Hope."

"What is that, exactly?"

"It's a place for abused women."

"And are you an abused woman?"

"Well, I been abused." Darlene looked down at her hands in her lap.

"Are you abused now?"

Darlene hesitated for a long minute. "I'm still suffering the effects of it. It doesn't just go away the minute they stop. But you probably wouldn't know anything about that. You being a big-time lawyer and all."

It took Vivian a minute to recover from the attack. She couldn't help but glance sideways at Walter.

"Are you employed?"

"Objection. Relevance." Walter was on his feet at the table across the aisle from Vivian.

"Relevance?" she asked, nonplussed. "Are you serious?"

"Overruled," the judge said. "Answer the question."

"No, ma'am. Not at this time, but—"

"Are you in school?"

"Objection."

Vivian crimped her lips and rolled her eyes at Walter. The muscles in her jaw tightened. Then she realized what Walter was doing. Just trying to throw her off stride. Old memories bubbled up. She took a deep breath.

"Your Honor, I believe it would be helpful for you to know as much as possible about this witness, what she is doing with her life, what she plans in terms of caring for the child, et cetera, so that you can make an informed decision. It would be obvious to an idiot—I mean, to anyone—that this information is relevant."

"Overruled. Answer the question."

"No. Not yet, but my—"

"Aren't you on felony probation?"

"Objection!" Walter interjected. "This is going too far."

"On what basis?" Vivian asked incredulously.

"Relevance, of course."

"How could anything be more relevant?"

"Counsel," the judge interjected. "Address your comments to me. Objection overruled. The witness should answer the question."

Darlene's shoulders slumped almost imperceptibly. "Yes, ma'am."

"How do you propose to take care of your daughter?"

"I haven't worked out all the details, but I know I can do it."

"Do you feel that Monee is safe, living with your mother?"

"Objection. Calls for speculation."

"That's not speculation. I asked her how she feels. The answer is obvious by the witness leaving her child with her mother. And you know it."

"Counsel," the judge admonished, "address yourself to me."

"Yes, Your Honor. I'm sorry," Vivian said.

"The witness should answer the question."

"Yes. But she would be safe living with me too. There are other children there."

"What about school? How would you get her there?"

"There's a bus that comes there to pick up the kids."

"Does that bus go to Monee's school?"

"Well, she'd have to change schools, I suppose."

"And do you think that's good for the child?"

"Lots of kids change schools nowadays."

"What if she gets sick? How would you pay for that, since you don't have a job?"

"That's easy. Mama has her on her insurance."

"What about clothes?"

"Monee has plenty clothes. She wouldn't need any for a while."

"And when she does?"

"I plan to be working by then."

"And if you're not?"

"Mama will buy her some clothes. She likes to see Monee looking pretty."

Vivian didn't say anything for a long time. Then she found her voice. "Young lady, your sense of entitlement absolutely astounds me. Pass the witness."

Walter waited for so long that they all turned to look at him. Finally, he sat up straight.

"Darlene, I only have a few questions to ask you and I want you to tell the truth, just like you did in my office."

"All right."

"Do you dispute the fact that your mother has had to take care of your daughter ever since her birth?"

"No, sir."

"Very good. How old were you when your child was born?"

"Sixteen."

"And how old are you now?"

"Twenty-five."

"Did you finish high school?"

"No, sir. But I did get my GED."

Bobbie cringed. She hoped that the judge was not looking at her. Here she was a so-called expert in education and her own child hadn't finished high school.

"Now, you told the judge that you are on probation. So you've run afoul of the law, right? You're not trying to hide that from the judge, are you?"

"No, sir, I've had a little trouble with the law. But I didn't murder nobody or nothing like that. It was just a little forgery case. This man wrote a check out to me and I cashed it. I had to give him half the money. I know I shouldn't have done it, but . . . well, I don't have an excuse. It was my fault. I was running with the wrong company. I'm getting my life straightened out now. I'm taking classes. I participate in the counseling groups. I'm doing everything right."

"And as part of you getting your life together, you want to assume your responsibilities, isn't that right?"

"Objection. Leading."

"Counselor, this is cross-examination. It's permissible for me to lead the witness."

Vivian seethed that he would presume to teach her the law.

"Continue, please," the judge said to Darlene.

"Yes, sir. I want to assume my responsibilities."

"And you appreciate all that your mother has done for you and your child, don't you?"

"Oh, yes, sir. Lord knows, my mama has had to put up with a lot from me. And I appreciate all she's done. Me and my baby could have never made it this far without her. But it's way past time for me to be Monee's mama. Before she gets too grown and all. And because of my experience, I think I can better help her to avoid the pitfalls that I didn't."

"Now, it's true that you're not working?"

"Well, sir, I'm not exactly working yet. But I'm looking real hard. And I'm following up on every lead that my case-worker gives me. It's kind of hard for a person like me to get a job. When people see probation on your record—and I always tell the truth about that—they just don't seem interested. It's like they think you're gonna steal from 'em. It's hard to convince them that you've turned your life around. I'm smart, real smart. But I don't have any skills to speak of. I'm not picky. I've even applied for jobs as a hotel maid. Couldn't get one, though. I think they like hiring those Mexican girls because they can treat them any kind of way and they know the girls won't report it. You know they're scared of being deported."

"But the main point here is that you do intend to have a job and you are willing to work."

"Oh, yes, sir. And soon as I get a job, I can get an apartment for me and Monee to live in."

"Now, Darlene, you love your daughter, don't you?"

"Oh, yes, sir."

"And you'll do anything the judge tells you to do, if you can have custody of her, won't you?"

Darlene turned to the judge with a wide-eyed, innocent look. "Ma'am, I'd do anything you say."

A lone woman joined the four of them in the elevator and they rode to the bottom floor in rigid silence. Walter and Darlene got off first, then Darlene turned to Bobbie and said, "I'll be by Friday around six to pick her up."

At that moment, Vivian took hold of Bobbie's hand and held it to her side. Her touch said so many things. Be cool. Don't answer. Let her go.

"It's just for the weekend, Bobbie."

17

BOBBIE STORMED up the stairs and threw herself across the bed. The pounding in her head echoed the sound of Ray's hammering downstairs. She couldn't think. Not that she wanted to. The judge's ruling had not been what she was expecting at all, although Vivian had tried to warn her. She marched back downstairs to the doorway of the kitchen.

"Can't you just stop making all that damn racket?"

Ray turned and looked at her, the smile fading from his face. "I thought I heard you come in. How'd it go?"

"Not good. Not good at all. Listen, I'm having a bad day. Can't you just leave off all this banging? It's giving me a headache."

"Just give me a minute here, I only have to—"

"No, you don't have to do a damn thing but be quiet. Why don't you go home. Can't I just have my house to myself for one day?"

Ray set the hammer down. "I'm sorry, Bobbie. You want to tell me about it?"

"No!"

"Tell me about it anyway."

Bobbie's lips tightened. "The judge said I have to give Monee to Darlene."

"When?"

"Friday. Tomorrow."

"Are you going to do it?"

"I have no choice. I don't want to go to—" Her voice broke, and she cupped her hands to her face to hide the warm tears that sprang from her eyes. She hated to break down in front of Ray, but she'd reached her breaking point.

Ray pulled her hands down, put his arms around her shoulders, and pressed her head against his chest. He leaned back, his weight against the counter, and held her to him. That seemed to make her cry harder, but he knew she needed the release, so he didn't try to stop her.

When he felt that the storm had spent itself, he said, "Tell me what happened." He tore a paper towel off the roll on the counter and handed it to her. She wiped her eyes, then sheepishly turned her head and blew her nose.

"I can't believe it. I'll bet that judge doesn't even have chick nor child. How the hell can she decide what's best for Monee? She didn't even care that I have been the one taking care of her. Like my sacrifice counts for nothing. It's just not fair. All she could talk about is the future. Well, Monee doesn't have a future with me? Like what kind of a future is she going to have with Darlene? Oh, she fussed Darlene out and threatened her—if she doesn't get herself together. I've already got myself together. Why would she play with this child's life that way? And now Monee's going to have to be in that terrible place. Even though it's just for the weekend, Monee's not used to that."

"How do you know it's terrible? Have you been there?"

"No, but I know it's not as nice as here."

Ray twisted his mouth and made a little sucking sound. He had to give her that one. "What about you letting them both live here?"

"I thought about that. Just to protect Monee. But I know Darlene hasn't changed. It would just be drama, drama, drama. Darlene would have all these unsavory types coming around. I'd have to start hiding things again."

"Again?"

Bobbie looked up at him. There was no point in keeping it from him any longer. "Darlene is more than just irresponsible. She's been on drugs. I can't trust her to live in my house."

"And the judge is giving the child to her?" He frowned hard.

"Darlene told the judge that she's off now. That she's getting her life together. And she was pretty convincing. All dressed up and looking normal. I know that sleazy lawyer of hers was behind that. Probably bought her those clothes. He tried to make me look bad."

"You? How could he make you look bad?"

Bobbie didn't want to tell him about the insinuation the lawyer had made about her being an unwed mother. She had worked so hard to correct her mistake. She thought she could overcome the stigma. Apparently it would always be there, even in her own mind. Still, she couldn't bring herself to tell him.

"Talking about me having a boyfriend. Humph." She folded her arms across her chest.

"You have a boyfriend?" Ray asked, a look of surprise on his face. "I didn't know you had a boyfriend. He sure doesn't come around much."

"I do *not* have a boyfriend. A woman my age doesn't have boyfriends," Bobbie said irritably.

"What does a woman your age have?"

"You sound like that lawyer."

"Maybe you need a boyfriend."

"I do *not* need a boyfriend."

"What do you need, Bobbie?"

She thought a long moment, staring at nothing. "I need a friend."

Ray put his knuckle under her chin and raised it for her to look at him. "Can I be your friend?"

Tears welled up in Bobbie's eyes, then spilled over and ran down her cheeks.

Ray pulled her to him and rubbed her back reassuringly. "You don't have to cry. It's not that bad having me for a friend."

Bobbie chuckled against his chest.

"Seriously," he said. "I know it's going to be hard on you, but you've got to obey the judge. Tell you what. Why don't you let me take you away this weekend. Otherwise, you're just going to be moping around here worrying about everything. I know just the place. Pack a little bag. I'll pick you up bright and early Saturday morning."

Friday evening, Bobbie stood on the porch and watched the old hoopty drive off, trailing a cloud of gray smoke. Darlene sat up front with Antonio. Bobbie couldn't believe Darlene had brought that shifty-eyed joker to her house. She'd always suspected him to be behind the Christmas-present heist. At least this time he'd had the decency to stay in the car.

Bobbie could see Monee in the backseat looking at her out of the back window. When they were at the corner, Bobbie could still hear the thudding boom-boom of the bass. Even if the loud music didn't burst Monee's eardrum, all that profanity was not good for her to hear. Bobbie shook her head and wondered what she could be charged with if she shot Antonio's tires out.

Finally she went in the house. She walked around in circles for a while, with her brow furrowed, thinking evil thoughts about the judge, Darlene, Walter Carlson, and her lawyer. Finally she knew she had to turn it over to the Lord, or else she was going to think herself straight to hell. Might as well do something useful to kill time until bedtime.

The evening was warm for early spring, so she left her jacket in the car when she parked in front of Autumn Oaks. She was so relieved that Mrs. Swink had stopped talking about going home. Bobbie had paid this month's rent with the cash she'd found in the house. She'd had the cable and the phone turned off and had stopped the newspaper. That would save a little money. Bobbie felt remiss because she still hadn't gotten the window fixed. But now there was no hurry. She had put a timer on the lamp so the house would appear occupied. And Mrs. Downs was keeping an eye on it for her. The grass hadn't started growing yet, but when it did, she could pay that boy down the street to keep it cut. Those damn roses would just have to see about themselves. Soon she would start talking to Mrs. Swink about selling the house. That way, she could afford to live in Autumn Oaks the rest of her life.

Mrs. Swink wasn't in her room again, but this time Bobbie wasn't panicked. She thought that she was lost in the building somewhere, she'd just have to look for her. Bobbie knew that the dining hall was closed, but she walked that way anyway. As she ran her hand along the polished wood railing on the wall, she thought again that this was the best place for Mrs. Swink. Every detail for the convenience and safety of the residents was seen to. Mrs. Swink would be well cared for here.

When she reached a padded bench, Bobbie sat down a minute and looked out onto the courtyard. She hoped that when she became old and feeble, she would be able to afford a nice place like this. Sure, it was a little depressing, and the thought of the big black station wagon Mr. Rafaeli had mentioned frightened her a little. On the other hand, three meals a day—cooked by someone else—and no responsibility for the upkeep of a house didn't seem like such a bad deal.

Out in the courtyard, she saw an old couple, both clad in sweaters, slowly walking. Despite their slow gait, the man was engaged in an animated explanation of something. The woman was, by turns, shaking her head in disapproval and nodding in agreement. Bobbie knew that more than a few married couples lived in the building. Some women were so lucky. This one had probably been with her man for fifty years. And no matter what trials and tribulations she'd gone through with him over all those years, she still had him. Thirty years ago, he may have been a gambler or a womanizer, but now he was comfort for the woman in her last years. When Bobbie thought of her last years, the bag lady who lived in the back corner of her mind began whispering to her. Walking the streets alone during the day, pushing a shopping cart. Sleeping in shelters or doorways at night. In reality, Bobbie knew that if things went as planned, she would own her house free and clear, and she'd have a decent retirement. But the bag lady was in the back of her mind, whispering to her.

The couple had reached a park bench on the other side of the courtyard, and the old man took the woman's hand, then ever so gently helped her to sit. He sat next to her and put his arm around her. Now that they were facing her, Bobbie's mouth fell open. Then she closed it. Couldn't be. She walked to the window at the other end of the hallway where she could get a better look. It was. She saw the door that opened onto the courtyard and started for it. When her hand was on the bar, she stopped. What could she do? What should she do? Leave well enough alone. She turned and walked to her car with a big smile on her face.

The next morning, the ringing of the doorbell awakened Bobbie. The clock said 6:27. She'd had three hours of fitful sleep. Then she remembered. She grabbed her robe. When she came out of her bedroom, she could see from the top of the stairs that Monee had beat her to the door. Ray stood in the foyer, looking up at her with a puzzled look on his face. As she walked downstairs, she said, "Monee, go back to bed. I'll be up in a minute."

From the foyer, she watched Monee walk upstairs and waited until she had gone through the door at the top of the stairs. Then she turned to Ray.

"I'm sorry. I can't go. I intended to call you early this morning, but I had a rough night."

Ray raised his eyebrows in a question.

Bobbie sighed. "I guess I'll have to tell you about it. Let's sit on the porch."

When they were seated in the swing, Ray said, "Bobbie, I know it's not my place to be in your business. But you can't win like this. You have to let the child go. The judge can hold you in contempt. You're just making the situation worse."

"It's worse than you think. I did let her go. It almost killed me. But I let her go. Darlene showed up here with that Antonio. I can't stand him. He's got shifty eyes. I still let her go. I had a bad feeling about it. But I went on and packed a little bag for today. And I was looking forward to our trip. But I was worried about Monee. Sure enough, around two this morning, the phone rang. It was Monee. She was crying. Said she was scared. Darlene and Antonio had taken her with them to some apartment in East Austin. Then they left her there with some other children, I guess while they went out partying. Monee was able to describe the apartment complex to me. I knew where it was. I went to pick her up. When I got there, Darlene and bubblehead Antonio were just coming back. We had quite a scene. There was no way on earth I was going to leave Monee with them. Darlene was telling me about the court order and threatening to call the police. I didn't care if the police came. I knew she wouldn't call them because that Antonio was high as a kite. I could see it in his eyes. Funny, I don't think Darlene was high. And she seemed to be put out with him, but she still let him bully her. But, dammit, I don't have to take that off him. You should have heard the way he talked to me. That boy just don't know. I grew up in the Fifth Ward. I've dealt with his kind before."

"What did you do?"

"I'm not going to tell you how I really acted." Bobbie smiled a little. "Let's just say that I told him how the cow eats the cabbage. Anyway, I can't do anything about Darlene being with him if she's going to be that stupid, but I *can* do something about Monee. I brought Monee home. It took half the night to calm her down. The child shouldn't be subjected to that. Anyway, I'm sorry that you got up so early, but I can't go with you today."

Ray kept the gentle motion of the swing going with a push of his foot. He didn't say anything for a while.

"Is your bag still packed?" he asked.

"Yes, but—"

"Pack Monee a bag. She can go with us."

"But—"

"What are you going to do today—if you stay here?"

"I don't know."

"She's already packed for the weekend. Just throw in a swimsuit. Get yours too. I'll wait here."

"Oh my gosh. Are we going in this?" Bobbie asked.

Ray smiled as he unlocked the door to the RV. "Your carriage awaits, ladies."

"This is nice. I've never been in one before," Bobbie said as she stepped up. Monee pressed in right behind her.

"Oh, look, Granny. It's like a little house. It has a little kitchen, just my size, Granny! It's even got a bathroom! Can

I sleep up there?" Monee jumped up on the couch and tried to pull herself up on the overhead bed.

"Just hold on, Monee. Mr. Caldwell will tell us—"

"Sit down, Monee. Don't put your shoes on the couch. When we get situated, you can go up there. For now, the bags go up there." He lifted her hot-pink rolling bag up, then Bobbie's canvas satchel. Ray eased around into the driver's seat.

"You have to put on your seat belt up here in the cab. Monee doesn't have to wear one back there." Ray pulled away from the curb and headed east on Highway 290.

"Lake Somerville is not too far. A little more than an hour. It's near Brenham. The fishing's good." Ray adjusted the rearview mirror and caught sight of Monee sitting on the couch, straight as a little soldier, a pout on her lips. He had been disappointed to find he wouldn't have Bobbie to himself, but as long as Monee was here, he did want her to enjoy the trip. He almost relented and let her go up top, but that would only teach her that pouting would get her her way. He had something else in mind. The next time he looked around, she was sitting on the floor, occupied with taking the dress off a Barbie doll. Doll clothes and shoes were scattered out all around her.

On the far side of Brenham, Ray pulled into the parking lot at the Blue Bell Creamery. "As soon as you pick up all those doll clothes and put them away, I have a surprise for you, Monee."

"But I'm playing with them."

"I guess you don't want a surprise, then."

Monee looked out the window. "This isn't a lake. What is a cream-ery, Granny?"

"It's a place where they make ice cream," Bobbie answered.

Monee quickly gathered up the dolls and clothes and stuffed them in her backpack.

After they took the tour of the famous creamery, Ray insisted that they eat their end-of-the-tour treat there, but he bought five pints of different flavors to take with them.

A short while later, they were at the campsite near the lake's edge. Ray parked and hooked up to water and electricity. He handed each of them a fishing rod from the back compartment, then got a tackle box and two campstools. When they got down to the lake, neither Bobbie nor Monee would bait their hooks, so Ray did it for them. Soon, Monee lost interest in fishing and went to play in the minnow bucket. Bobbie's catching a fish rekindled Monee's interest, and luckily she got a bite too. Ray stood by to help her, but she did most of it herself.

"You ladies catch just one more and we can have lunch," Ray said.

Back at the campsite, Ray set out two chairs and a chaise lounge, then he set about cleaning the fish on the picnic table.

"Can I do something to help?" Bobbie asked from the chaise lounge.

"Not a thing. I just want you to relax and enjoy yourself."

"But I feel so useless."

"Good. Enjoy it."

Monee sat on the table and watched, fascinated, as he scaled, beheaded, and filleted their catch. Then he went inside the RV, rinsed, seasoned, and put the fish in the oven.

"Monee, come help me," he said from the doorway. "Carry these things to the table for me."

She made several trips with plates, napkins, serving utensils, a bowl of potato salad, and a bowl of green salad. The last thing he gave her was a plastic tumbler filled with ice and a soft drink. Then he brought out a bottle of wine and two glasses and set them on the table.

When the fish was done, Ray filled their plates and they ate heartily.

Bobbie could hardly keep her eyes open.

"Why don't you go stretch out on the bed and take a little nap. Monee and I can try to catch a few more fish to take back."

"I think I will," she said.

When Bobbie left, Monee said, "I don't want to catch any more stupid fish. It's boring."

Ray twisted his mouth. "What would you like to do, then?"

"I want to go inside and play with my dolls."

"No. Let your grandmother enjoy her nap. Let's go for a walk. We can find some wood and build a fire."

They walked along the edge of the lake.

"I hear you had a rough night."

Monee didn't say anything.

The wood was sparse, but they carried pieces they found back to the campsite, then went back for more. At the water's edge, Ray stopped for a large piece. He turned it over and examined it. "We won't put this one in the fire. This is a beautiful piece."

"No, it's not. It's ugly," Monee said.

"Beauty is not always on the outside. With a little time and attention, the beauty can come out."

"It's ugly. It's got knots and things on it. We should burn it too."

"I don't think so. See this knot right here? It looks like the man in the moon."

Monee bent over and looked at it. "That's not the man in the moon."

"I can make something pretty from this."

"You can't make anything pretty out of this old wood."

Ray just smiled.

The sun was on the low side when Bobbie came out of the RV. The fire was crackling, and Monee stood poking at it with a long stick she'd found.

"Don't you think it's about time for us to head on back?" Bobbie asked.

"No, Granny. I don't want to leave. Can't we stay here?"

"We have church in the morning."

"But, Granny, I want to stay. We can go to church any-time. Please? Can't we stay? We can pray here. And you can sing. It'll be just like church. It'll be even better. And I have my pajamas. And clean panties. And there's beds in there."

Bobbie looked at Ray for help.

"There's beds in there," he said. "And we could leave early enough in the morning for you to go to church. Or we can have church out here, like Monee said. 'Whenever two or more gather in My name . . .' "

"Yeah, Granny, that's what my Sunday-school teacher says. Please?"

"You're not being helpful here, Ray."

"I'm trying to be," he said with a smile.

The fire was down to a soft red glow. As on many nights before, Ray sat in the chair watching it. He'd sat here by himself many times. A few times, he'd sat here with his army buddies, retired guys like himself who had made it. They shared bawdy jokes to keep from sharing how they felt about the price they'd paid for making it. But this night was different. He felt something like a glow inside himself. Maybe it was the feminine influence. He had never brought a woman with him before. He'd enjoyed having Bobbie with him and had more than once thought that one day there might be a trip with just the two of them. But he'd enjoyed having the little girl too.

Earlier when they were all outside, there was a rustling in the leaves under a nearby tree, then a possum skittered through their campsite. Wide-eyed with fright, Monee had dashed to Ray and grabbed him around his waist. Right then, with her head buried against his ribs and his arm around her shoulders, he would have arm-wrestled Mike Tyson to protect her. Later, he and Bobbie had a good laugh at Monee's expense. Monee denied that she had been scared, but was suddenly sleepy and wanted to go to bed.

Now Ray turned and looked at the RV. The lights were out. When Bobbie had finally agreed to stay, he had offered them the big bed at the back, but Monee begged to sleep in the one over the cab. He'd told them to draw the curtain for a little privacy and that he would wait until they turned out the light before he came inside. He would undress in the dark, and he knew he would be up and dressed before they awoke in the morning.

Ray picked up three little dolls Monee had left in the chair next to his and walked to the RV.

18

TUESDAY NIGHT, Ray was in his workshop, listening to the oldies show on KAZI, the local community radio station. Ray rubbed his hand over the top of the little box he had made from the ugly wood. Once the finish had cured, he intended to line it with blue velvet. A perfect box for a little girl's jewelry, he thought with a satisfied smile. He gathered up the tack cloths that he'd used to wipe all traces of sawdust from the box's surface and stuffed them in a plastic bag. He was reaching for the can of boiled linseed oil when he felt a presence. He quickly turned around and saw Sonny.

"Boy, what are you doing here?" he asked. The sight of his son brought a big grin to his face.

"Just in the neighborhood. Thought I'd drop in."

"Bullshit. Kansas City is a long way from this neighborhood. Come on in. I'm glad to see you. Why didn't you call and let me know you were coming?" Ray rubbed his hands

on his jeans, then hugged his son. "Never mind, let's go in
the house. Where's Myrna and the kid?"

"They couldn't come this time. I came by myself. My
company sent me." Sonny looked away from Ray, took a
breath, then said, "Rasheed had a basketball game. His team
is in the finals."

"Well, it must have been something really important to
your company for you to miss his game," Ray said, putting
his arm around Sonny's shoulder.

"He's only five, Dad. It's real junior league."

Inside, Ray went to the refrigerator, retrieved two beers,
and handed Sonny one. "Come on in the den. Boy, it's sure
good to see you."

Ray sat in the recliner and clicked the TV on with the
remote. Sonny sat on the couch. The noise of a baseball
game that neither of them was interested in provided the
background.

"How was your flight? Are you hungry? I can—"

"Nah. Thanks, Dad. I ate in Waco."

"So you drove?"

"Yeah."

"That big company made you miss your son's game, and
they can't afford a flight and a rental car? Don't let them take
advantage of you, Son. A boy needs his daddy at a time like
that."

"I know, Dad. I know. But one of our clients is located
here. They're having some trouble with the books, and the
firm sent their star accountant to check it out. It'll only be a
few days. Maybe a week."

"What hotel are they putting you up in? I know that one
downtown on Cesar Chavez is really fine."

"I thought I'd stay with you while I'm here. Is that okay?"

"Well, of course. I'm glad to have the company. Maybe if they don't work you too hard, and you have a little spare time, we can hit some balls. There's a new golf course I've been wanting to try. So how is Myrna?"

Sonny hesitated so long that Ray looked at him.

"Aw, she's okay. You know Myrna is Myrna." Sonny let out a little chuckle. Ray's chuckle joined Sonny's as he nodded his head.

Ray liked Myrna. She looked a lot like Loretta, but she had a temperament more like his own. From the day Sonny had first brought her home, Ray had believed she was good for Sonny. She stood on solid feet, focused on the future. She worked hard and didn't mind sacrificing the now for a much better day. Ray understood that.

Ray yawned. "I think I'm going to turn in. Come on, you can bring your suitcase in the front bedroom. The sheets are clean."

"That's all right, Dad. I think I'll watch the game for a while. I'm a little hyped from the long drive. You go on. I'll catch you in the morning."

"Make sure you go by and see your grandmother while you're here."

Sonny had said he would be here a week. That would mean Tuesday. But this was Thursday. The only thing he'd said was that the set of books he was working on had turned out to be more complicated than expected—and even that he'd said in a rush to get out the door. He had left early each morning, going to his job. By the time Ray was finished for the evening, Sonny still wasn't back. He didn't know when Sonny returned. They had really been kind of passing each other and never really hooking up. They still hadn't gone to play golf.

Ray left his shop for a midmorning break and saw Sonny's car still in the driveway. It was ten already. Ray knocked on the guest-room door, but there was no answer. He opened the door and saw Sonny sprawled on the bed, still in his clothes. Ray called his name and Sonny jumped up as though he'd heard a shot.

"Jeez. Look at the time. I've got to get outta here." Sonny rushed to the shower.

"Will you have to work late?" Ray asked through the door. He didn't hear the mumbled reply. "I'd like to take you by and introduce you to a friend. I'll look for you around eight."

Ray went back to his shop to get his heavy-duty drill and his electric hammer. Today he was going to install the cabinet bases at Bobbie's house. It irked him no end that neither of the tools was where it was supposed to be. He looked all around the shop. He couldn't exactly remember the last time he'd used either of them. Maybe he'd left them at Bobbie's. No, he would remember that. Or would he? A bout of forgetfulness had attacked him lately, and he found himself making lists to help him remember little details.

Ray didn't think of himself as old, but then again, he certainly wasn't young. The thought of getting old scared him a little. He thought again of the newsletter he'd received last week from Ken, listing their army buddies who had passed, the ones who had cancer, another stricken by Parkinson's.

In his mind, all of them were too young for those kinds of afflictions. Agent Orange maybe? He tried to blow it off, but he couldn't. His tools had to be at Bobbie's. In all the days of his going in and out of her house, he'd carried a lot of them over there.

That night, Sonny drove into the driveway at seven forty-five. Ray appreciated that he had come on time, especially when he saw how bleary-eyed Sonny looked. He imagined that staring at numbers on a page all day would have that effect. No, these days it would be numbers on a computer screen. Even worse, Ray thought.

"This won't take long. I just wanted my friend to meet you before you leave," Ray said.

"I'll follow you in my car. I have to go back to the office for an hour or so. Going in late this morning really put me behind."

"You timed this just right," Bobbie said. "I haven't been in from choir practice but twenty minutes. Just long enough to get Monee to bed. She did her homework at the church. Y'all come on in."

"Bobbie, this is Sonny."

"Pleasure to meet you," she said, extending her hand. "I could tell you were Ray's son anywhere. Your dad told me you were here, doing a big job for an accounting firm. Come on, let's sit down."

Ray's face was covered with pride. "Yep. They've had him working night and day ever since he got here. He even has to go back to work tonight. But I wanted him to meet you before he leaves, so he made time. That's my boy."

"Have you eaten? I can rustle up some leftovers."

"No, don't bother. I ate a burger earlier and—"

"I ate at the office," Sonny said.

"Well, what about a drink?" she asked.

"I'll have whatever you're having," Ray said.

"You got a gin and tonic?" Sonny asked.

"Sorry, I don't have tonic water. What about orange juice?"

"That sounds good."

Bobbie fixed the drinks and set them on napkins on the coffee table.

"How long will be you be here, Sonny?" Bobbie asked. "Maybe I can have you over for a real dinner."

"Uh, I'm not sure right now. This was supposed to be a short trip, but I don't think I can get this thing wrapped up before Saturday."

"I was telling your dad that I'm surprised you didn't go in the military."

"Naw. Too regimented for me. I wouldn't have been able to stand that. I had enough just growing up in it."

Ray looked crestfallen. "It was good enough to get you where you are now." He folded his arms across his chest.

"I didn't mean any insult, Dad. The army was good to you. You enjoyed it. I just don't think I would. I'm not cut out for it."

"I wasn't cut out for it either, boy. I did what I had to do to make the most out of my life."

"Well, we each have to follow our own paths," Bobbie broke in, trying to bring the conversation back to the pleasant side. "Do you like accounting?"

"Not as much as I thought I would. I was raised to believe that everything should be neat and orderly. Accounting is like that. But you know, it just kind of makes me mad. All day long, I'm counting other people's money. Some people have a whole lot of it. I can slave away in a cubicle at the firm for years and never have that kind of money."

Bobbie and Ray both noticed that Sonny's glass was empty. She offered him another. He accepted. When Bobbie handed it to him, the doorbell rang. "Excuse me a minute."

When Bobbie looked through the peephole, she didn't want to open the door, but that would seem strange to her guests. And besides, Darlene would probably ring again and wake Monee up, so she opened it.

"Darlene?"

"Hi, Mama." Darlene looked repentant. Bobbie didn't say anything. Her lips tightened, her head crooked in a question.

"I was hoping . . . I guess you're mad at me."

Bobbie didn't answer.

"Can I see Monee just a minute? I wanted to explain to her—"

"Monee's gone to sleep. She has school in the morning."

Darlene looked down. "I caught the last bus over here. Could you loan me twenty dollars for a taxi?"

Bobbie was between a rock and a hard place. She had sworn she wouldn't give Darlene money. Still, she didn't want her child walking the streets this time of night. And there was no way she was going to have Darlene in the house overnight. Even though she was dressed nicely and her hair was combed, Bobbie didn't trust her. The last time she had, she'd lost her new portable phone; the time before, it was the little TV. Darlene might be able to fool that judge, but Bobbie had experience. "Just a minute."

Bobbie went back through the living room on her way to the kitchen to get her purse. "I'll be with you in a minute. I need to call a cab for my daughter."

"Your daughter is here? I'd like to meet her," Ray said, standing expectantly.

Although she'd told him about Darlene, she couldn't bring herself to tell him she wouldn't let Darlene in her house. "She's kind of in a hurry."

"Well, it wouldn't take but a minute just to meet her," he insisted.

Bobbie walked back to the door with a new worry. Would Darlene tell her lawyer about Ray? She opened the door to let Darlene in. "Come on in. A friend of mine wants to meet you."

Bobbie didn't invite Darlene to sit. "Ray, this is my daughter, Darlene. Sonny, Darlene. Darlene is just leaving. I'll be right back."

"Where are you going?" Sonny asked. "I'm just about to leave too. I can give you a lift." He set his empty glass on the coffee table. "Ms. Strickland, I'm glad I got a chance to meet you. Thanks for the drink. Dad, I'll check you later."

Ray and Bobbie stood at the door, his arm around her shoulder, watching their children walk to Sonny's car. Neither said anything for a long time. Both were lost in their own thoughts. Ray thought Darlene didn't look like a drug addict. Bobbie wondered what Sonny was going to lose behind that ride.

Finally, Ray broke the silence. "Guess I'd better go. You've got school in the morning."

Bobbie nodded her agreement, although she was really enjoying the nearness of him. Ray lifted her chin and touched his lips to hers. When she didn't resist, he gave her a full-blown kiss. They were both surprised, but then they really weren't. Bobbie fit perfectly against him. She felt his hands rubbing her back. It had been a long time since she'd wanted a man. Really wanted a man, the way she wanted this man right now. She could tell he wanted her too. She wanted to take him upstairs to her big bed and . . . but Monee was upstairs. Bobbie reluctantly broke from his embrace.

19

Ray was too restless and agitated to go to bed. He wasn't accustomed to feeling this way. He didn't feel like working in his shop. Nothing on TV interested him, so he wandered aimlessly around the house. Everywhere he stopped, he straightened up a little bit. When he found himself arranging the pencils in his desk drawer, he tried to stop himself. He could still smell Bobbie's cologne. Maybe he should pleasure himself so that he could go to sleep. No. That was beneath him. He thought about calling Jocelyn. He'd had a little sumpin-sumpin with her a while back. But that wouldn't be satisfying. And it wouldn't be fair to Jocelyn. He made another circle, then he heard Sonny's car in the driveway.

Sonny looked surprised to see Ray still up.

"Did you get Darlene home okay?" Ray asked.

"Yep. I'm really tired. I'm going to turn in."

"Hold up a minute, Sonny. Myrna hasn't called since

you came. I was hoping to holler at her. Is something going on?"

"Going on, like what?" Sonny asked, his eyes wide in feigned innocence.

Ray had seen that look for more than twenty years and knew better.

"Sit down, boy. Something's wrong. You can tell me."

Sonny sat. Even though he was a grown man, he was accustomed to following his father's orders. He looked everywhere except in Ray's eyes.

"That's why I'm here, actually. She's gone crazy."

"Myrna?"

"Yeah."

Ray's brow furrowed in confusion. "Lil' Myrna? Crazy how?"

"I don't know what's wrong with her. She made me move out of the house."

"Your house? What brought that on?"

"I don't know. She said I wasn't giving her what she needed."

Ray let that thought roll around in his head. He'd heard it before.

"Like what?"

"I don't know. She's just crazy. And after all I've done for her. Put her through school. Worked my butt off, giving her all the stuff she wanted. Bought that house I could barely afford. She dresses that kid in designer jeans. She just has no idea how much ass I had to kiss to get a promotion to afford all that. Those people on her job are jumping her up and down, swelling her head. Now she feels like she doesn't need me."

It all sounded familiar to Ray. Felt familiar. His heart went out to Sonny. He was so young. And his kid was so young. Ray wanted to comfort him, but he didn't know the words to say without saying something ugly about Loretta. He had never expressed his feelings about Loretta or the divorce to the boys. All of that was between the two of them. Even at his angriest, he had had to admit that Loretta had been a good mother. He saw a tear fall down Sonny's face and was embarrassed for him.

"It's not manly to cry, Son."

Sonny angrily wiped the tear away. "I know, Dad. But it just makes me so mad. I could just choke that . . . her."

"Now, you can't do that. That'll cause you a lot more problems than you already have."

"I know, I know. You just don't know how it feels. I came home and found two suitcases on the porch. Just like I was a boarder who hadn't paid his rent. She changed the locks on the door. I didn't know what else to do. I just came here."

"It's all right, Sonny. Just take your time. You can stay here until you work this out."

Saturday night, Ray stood on the porch wishing he had bought a pretty package to put the box in. He hoped that his plan would work. He thought he'd built enough trust that it just might. When Bobbie opened the door, he shifted the plain brown sack to his other hand.

"I'm here to see Monee."

Curiosity raised Bobbie's eyebrows. "Come on in. She's in the living room watching TV."

"Would you mind giving us a little privacy? I'll tell you all about it later."

Bobbie gave him a questioning look, but acquiesced to the assurance he'd given her. "I've got to put icing on a cake I made for the bake sale. Come on back when y'all finish.

"Monee, you've got company." Then Bobbie went into the kitchen.

"Hey, Mr. Ray," Monee said.

Ray walked in and sat on the couch near where Monee sat on the floor.

"I brought you something."

Monee perked up when she saw the sack. She moved to the couch. "What is it?"

"Something you wanted." Ray handed the sack to her. Monee opened it and took the box out, looked it over, and set it in her lap. She ran her hand over the smooth top.

"I made it for you."

"It's pretty."

"Open it."

When she lifted the lid, she pressed her lips in a tight smile, then looked up at him. "It's the man in the moon. And it's not ugly anymore."

"Told ya." The excitement in Monee's eyes brought a smile to his face.

"It's for me?"

Ray nodded.

"Can I put anything in it I want to?"

"Sure."

"I'm gonna put something special in it. Something my mama gave me."

"Well, first I need something from you."

Monee looked at him.

"Something's been bothering me. You know your grandmother and I have become pretty good friends, right?"

Monee nodded.

"And I think you and I have become pretty good friends too, right?"

She smiled and nodded again.

"The thing that's bothering me is that I feel like I'm helping you keep a secret from her. And friends don't do that."

Monee looked wary.

"So, I thought that since you won't tell her about your secret with Antonio, maybe you'd tell me."

Monee shook her head.

"After what happened the last time, I don't think Antonio is your friend. Remember how scared you were that night your grandmother came to get you?"

A worried look crossed Monee's face at the remembrance.

"Have I ever done anything to scare you?"

She shook her head.

Ray waited.

Finally she looked up at him. "Granny will punish me. It was something wrong."

Ray fought to keep the worry that he felt off his face. If it turned out to be what he was thinking now, Bobbie wouldn't forgive him for not telling her sooner. He had been derelict. Still, he had to get it out of Monee now, so he used his soothing voice.

"But she will still love you. And I will still be your friend." He waited.

"You promise?"

Ray nodded.

"One time, we went in this record store. It was me, and Mama, and Antonio. When Mama wasn't looking, Antonio put two CDs in my backpack. And he didn't even pay for them. He said it was okay because the store had lots of them and wouldn't miss those two. He gave me the one of Destiny's Child, and he kept the other one." She searched Ray's face for his reaction.

Ray's shoulders almost slumped with relief. "And you knew that was wrong, didn't you?"

"Yes, sir. But I didn't even play it. I hid it under my bed so Granny wouldn't see it. And I prayed over it at church that Sunday. Please don't tell her, Mr. Ray."

"I guess since I'm your friend, and I'm her friend, and I don't want her to be hurt, it's best not to tell her—this one time."

Monee's face flushed with relief.

"Why don't you go put something in your box now."

Monee scooted off the couch and ran to the stairs. She stopped on the first step.

"Thank you, Mr. Ray. I like it. I like it a lot. It's a lot better than that one at the Home Center." Then she skipped up the stairs.

Ray walked into the kitchen and gave Bobbie a kiss on the back of her neck. She turned and gave him a shy one on the lips. "Stick your tongue out." When he did, she put a finger of icing on it.

"That's good. Lemon?"

She nodded. "You know I'm curious. What's all the secrecy with you and Monee?"

Ray wondered if she had been listening at the door, but decided she couldn't have heard them. "Oh, it's nothing. I made a little box for her. She went to her room to put something special in it."

"You're so sweet." Bobbie went back to icing the cake.

Ray sat at the kitchen table watching Bobbie work at the counter. Their conversation was comfortable and easy. The sounds of cartoons wafted from the living room television. He could get used to this. It reminded him of what he had liked about being married.

"Ray, I'd like it if you'd go to church with us tomorrow."

Ray took a sip from the tall, frosty glass of orange juice she'd handed him. "Are you singing?"

"Yes. But not a solo."

"Why don't you just sing a solo for me now. Right here. That would be enough religion for me."

"I'm serious. I want you to come."

He took another sip. "Maybe."

Bobbie could see there was no point in pressing him, so she dropped it for now. But just for now.

"Have you ever thought about getting old?" Ray asked.

"I haven't had time to think about that. Why are you thinking about it?"

"Well . . . it seems like lately . . . it's nothing."

"Doesn't seem like nothing to me."

"Do you worry about your mind going?"

"Going where?" When she saw the perturbed look on his face, Bobbie pursed her lips. "No. You think your mind is going?"

"I can't find some of my tools. I thought they were over here, but the cabinets are finished. And I've taken everything home."

"Maybe you put them in a different place."

He shook his head. "Why would I put them in a different place when there is a place made just for each one of them?"

"I don't know. Got distracted, maybe?"

"Maybe," he said, unconvinced.

"Nothing's different from when I met you. Except Sonny is here. Maybe he moved them."

"Naw, he hasn't been around the shop. Never took a liking to it."

"It's only normal to be a little forgetful. I wouldn't worry about it."

"Yeah, you wouldn't."

Bobbie turned to look at him. "What's that supposed to mean?"

"Nothing. I didn't mean anything."

"Yes, you did. What?"

Ray hesitated. "Well, just look at this place. You let Monee leave things everywhere. And after I put those organizers in the cabinets and drawers, you still just throw things in there willy-nilly."

"I can find what I need," Bobbie said defensively. "And Monee's just a child. She should be able to enjoy her childhood. She's not in the army."

"A little army wouldn't hurt her," he said offhandedly.

The clanking of the top Bobbie slammed on the pot startled Ray. "It didn't seem to do your son a lot of good."

"What's my son got to do with Monee being messy?"

"The way he sucked down those drinks the other night should be more your concern than my grandchild."

"I can see you're in a mood. I'd better go."

"Uh-huh. You can dish it out all right, but you can't take it."

20

RAY WANDERED aimlessly around his shop. He rearranged his cans of stain in precise chromatic order—honey ash on one end, deep mahogany on the other. He fretted that he couldn't find his drill and electric hammer, and he'd exhausted looking in all the places they could possibly be. But mostly he still stung from what Bobbie had said about Sonny. Just because a man has a couple of drinks after a hard day's work doesn't make him a drunk. And the boy had a lot on his mind. Ray sensed the defensiveness in himself. Perhaps she was entitled to be a little defensive about Monee too. Maybe she was just getting back at him. Tit for tat. He thought about going to her house to get things straight. They shouldn't let their children come between them. But what if she turned him away? He wouldn't be able to stand that. He thought about calling her. No, she should call him. She was the one who had escalated the fight. What could he do now? Ray didn't like feeling confused and unsettled. Certainty and order had ruled his life. He knew just the thing to restore his peace of mind.

Ray put four eggs, a quart of orange juice, and a package of turkey bacon in a plastic bag. He carried it out to the RV and put it in the little refrigerator with the intention of driving to the lake near Fort Hood. Just an hour's drive, a few hours' sleep, and a little early-morning fishing would cure him. He went back to the house for a few beers and to lock up. All the beer was gone, and he realized that Sonny was too.

Back inside the RV, he spotted one of Monee's dolls on the couch, then another doll and three tiny high-heeled shoes on the floor under the chair. He sat on the couch, holding the little dolls in his hands. He fit two of the shoes on one doll. He put the remaining shoe on the other doll, then searched for its mate. The least she could have done, if she just had to junk up his RV, was to lose a matching pair. The thought struck him as ridiculous. As ridiculous as expecting a child to be as orderly as he had become with twenty-five years of practice in the army.

He sat there a long time, thinking back over his life. The sacrifices he'd made in all those years had almost paid off. But he had lost his wife—and half of the retirement he'd worked for. He'd found control, found quiet, found peace, but not joy—until he met Bobbie. Her excitement when she first saw the new cabinets had brought joy to his heart. The way Monee's face had lit up when she saw the man in the moon in the lid of the jewelry box had brought joy to his heart. Ray drifted into a fitful sleep wondering if he could be satisfied with the kind of existence he'd had before.

Morning sunlight streaming through the window woke

him. The next thing he knew, he was showered, suited up, and driving to Mt. Moriah.

From the choirstand, Bobbie saw Ray slip into the church and sit near the back. He seemed to look everywhere except at her, but she knew he was sneaking a peek. She suppressed the pleased smile that bubbled up inside her before it reached her face. She was supposed to be mad at him. All night she had fumed about it—especially while she took all the pots and pans out of the cabinet and put them back, in order. In fact, she had had some uncharitable thoughts about him this very morning, and in the house of the Lord. Maybe she shouldn't have insinuated that his son was a drunk. She didn't even know the boy. But when he'd attacked Monee, she'd just lost it.

Ray thought she looked beautiful, standing with the other identically robed singers. He'd missed her. And it hadn't even been one day. He hadn't realized how much a part of his life she'd become.

Toward the end of the adult service, the children filed in from their separate service and filled in the back two rows. Monee spotted Ray and came over and sat next to him. He patted her knee in greeting. She looked up at him and smiled.

Ray looked around the church, at the stained-glass windows that had been in the old church, at the new pews, at his mother standing in the side aisle with her white-gloved hands folded in front of her. I could get used to this, he thought.

When the service was over, Ray and Monee waited in the

vestibule for Bobbie. Ray saw his mother bustling toward him. She gave him a hug.

"I'm so glad you came. The Lord must be whispering to you, to keep you off the lake this morning," she said with a big grin. "Who's your little friend?"

"This is Monee. You know Bobbie Strickland, don't you? Monee's her granddaughter. I'm hoping they'll let me take them to dinner. You want to go with us?"

Ray saw recognition, then puzzlement, then an understanding smile cross his mother's face.

"Wouldn't miss it for the world," she said. "No wonder you haven't been around much lately. You've been keeping secrets from your ol' mama." She gave him a knowing smile. "Bobbie Strickland is a fine woman. Good, God-fearing woman. Oh, there's Bobbie now."

Monee ran to greet her. Bobbie tightened her lips to keep her smile from showing how happy she was to see Ray. He didn't try to hide his.

"Granny, Mr. Caldwell is going to take us all out to dinner. Can we go to McDonald's?"

Before Bobbie could answer, Brother Harris walked up wearing an exuberant grin that showed his gold tooth. He grabbed Ray's hand and pumped it.

"Brother Caldwell. So good to see you this morning. Since you're coming to church kind of regular, and apparently keeping company with one of our good sisters"— Harris's eyebrow raised in a knowing gesture—"it's time for you to get involved. The Lord don't need no mo' bench-warmers. You need to join our prison ministry."

Ray pulled his hand back as politely as he could. He couldn't keep his eye off Brother Harris's earring.

"We need strong brothers such as yourself to reclaim our young warriors from Satan's grip. No coward soldiers in my God's army. We gather here at the church on Wednesdays at six-thirty, then drive the van out to the facility. Can we look for you this Wednesday?"

"I'll see" was Ray's noncommittal reply. "Right now, I'm taking these ladies to dinner. If you'll excuse us . . ."

"You need to step up to the plate, Brother."

As Brother Harris walked away, Ray frowned. There was something about the man he didn't like. Too pushy. An odor lingered about him that Ray couldn't quite place, but he didn't like it. He couldn't imagine being trapped up in a van with him. Sunday service was one thing, but he was through being a soldier.

Then he smiled at Bobbie. "I invited Mama too. The truck will be too cramped. Can we go in your car? You name the place."

When they got to Bobbie's car, she and Monee piled all her junk on the floor on one side in the backseat. Ray offered his mother the front seat, but she declined.

"I'll sit back here with Ms. Monee."

The church was in the historically black part of town, mere blocks from the Capitol, but neglected by the city for years. The surrounding neighborhood had pockets of gentrification, other homes that had been cared for for years, but for the most part it was deteriorated and run-down. Some of the houses were boarded up and abandoned—except by the drugheads. All through dinner, Mrs. Caldwell teased them about getting together without her permission. From the smile on her face, she was obviously pleased about it.

"Mama, has Sonny been by to see you?" Ray asked, trying to change the subject.

"Oh, yes. He's come by a couple of times. The boy still eats like a horse," she chuckled. "And he loves Grama's cooking. Seems like he can't get enough of it—he mentioned that he's thinking of moving here."

"Really? Did he mention how Myrna feels about that?" Ray was careful not to tell her any more than she knew.

"No. He didn't mention Myrna at all. Surely it's something they've discussed."

"I'll bet they have," he agreed.

After dinner, Bobbie drove them back to the church to get their vehicles. She stopped first at the parking lot across the street and let Mrs. Caldwell out at her car. Then she drove Ray a block away to his truck.

"If you don't have any plans, I'd like to come over later," he said. "Get a little swinging in."

"That would be fine." Bobbie smiled at the prospect.

When she reached the block that brought her to the stop sign across from church, she saw Reverend Jackson coming out of the side door of his office. Now was the perfect time to talk with him about having a fund-raiser for some new things that were needed in the church kitchen. The Lexus wasn't in his parking spot, and he was walking briskly down the street. She pulled alongside him near the end of the block, but it wasn't Reverend Jackson. She rolled the window down to call his name, but he kept walking and she didn't really have anything to say to Trey anyway.

★   ★   ★

Bobbie wore a gauzy hostess gown she'd bought months ago in an impulsive moment of foolish extravagance. At the time, she'd had nowhere to wear it and no one to wear it for. Tonight was the perfect occasion. She had spent the evening straightening up the house, filing papers away, helping Monee to put her toys in their proper places. She tried to deny that she was doing it because Ray was coming over. It was just time to get some of those things done, she told herself. But she knew better.

After Monee had gone to bed, Bobbie realized how late it was and wondered if he was coming. She almost called him, but she had been trained to let the man call her. So she sat down at the dining room table with the evaluation forms for her teachers. They were due next week, but it wouldn't hurt to get a jump on them. For most of her staff, the task would be easy. Most of her teachers were seasoned veterans who had an ingrained dedication to the children, and they would get superior evaluations. Even the three new ones whom she'd had reservations about at the beginning of the year had passed muster. Because they were right out of college and white at that, she hadn't expected them to stay a semester. She had thought they would ask for transfers, like the two she had last year. But these had shown their mettle and had earned the superior ranking she put on their forms. Two or three teachers, she knew, would not like their evaluation. They were disgruntled in faculty meetings, uncooperative with her, and showed their disdain for the students and their parents. For those she would recommend a transfer. She owed that to the children. When she got to Bill Gibson, she had to think long and hard. It was much more difficult to get an assistant principal moved. If she expressed her true feel-

ings, the administration would instruct her to counsel him
and work with him. She'd been there, done that. If she gave
him a superior evaluation, maybe they'd move him to
another school. But would that be fair to another principal?
She decided to sleep on his and stacked the papers to put in
her briefcase.

When she heard a soft knocking on the door, she looked
at her watch. Ten o'clock. She opened the door, but no one
was there. It immediately occurred to her how foolish she'd
been to open it without checking first. Even so, curiosity
made her step on the porch and look around. Ray was sitting in the swing.

"What took you so long?" he asked.

"I was going to ask you the same thing." She closed the
door behind her and joined him on the swing.

"That dress is beautiful on you."

She smiled. "Thank you."

"I guess since my mama has peeped my hole card, I can
put my arm around you." He did it without waiting for her
permission.

Bobbie enjoyed the lulling motion of the swing, and the
warmth of his arm around her shoulder.

"Another thing. I've decided that I want to be your
boyfriend. Or whatever a woman your age has."

Bobbie didn't say anything. Not because she didn't want
him to be, but because she'd always thought that a commit-
ted relationship should be built on honesty, and she hadn't
been honest with him.

"I'm not interested in a here-today, gone-tomorrow kind
of thing," she finally said.

"I've been here for quite a while now."

"That you have," she acknowledged, remembering all the days she'd come home from work to find him working in the kitchen.

"So? What about it?"

"Well, there's Monee. I intend to have her until she's grown. I don't care what that judge says."

"Okay. I figured that. What else?"

Bobbie hesitated, but if he was serious, he needed to know it all. And if it would make a difference to him, she needed to know now.

"I've never been married."

Ray didn't say anything for a long time. "Are you proposing?"

"No, of course not," she said almost too quickly.

"Oh, so I'm not worthy of carrying your name?" he asked, still teasing.

His lightheartedness gave her the perfect opportunity to turn back. She could just give him a teasing rejoinder and move on to something else. But that would only postpone the inevitable.

Her voice was quiet and low. "I carry my father's name. I have two children. And a grandchild. And we all carry my father's name."

The teasing smile fell from Ray's face. His voice took on a serious tone. "So there are two men out there somewhere who betrayed their manhood, and who didn't live up to their responsibility. What does that have to do with me? With us?"

Bobbie looked into his eyes for a long time. Ray's gaze didn't waver. Then Ray pressed his lips to hers.

21

MONDAY MORNING, Bobbie felt as if she were walking on a cloud. She didn't really know what to do with this new feeling that she had. The grass looked greener, but that was just the ripening of spring. The sky was a prettier blue than she'd remembered. But that was just the season too. Idalia even smiled and waved at her as she pulled out of her driveway.

She should have known it couldn't last. Before first period was over, Mrs. Brown showed up at her door with DeShawn. Bobbie's heart sank. She knew it was rock-and-a-hard-place time—caught between the district's removal policy and the district lawyer's advice.

"What is it, Mrs. Brown?" Bobbie asked, dreading the answer.

Mrs. Brown urged a reluctant DeShawn into the office. "DeShawn has been acting out all morning. When I tried to speak with him about it, he used profanity with me. I can't tolerate that in my classroom. So I took him in the hallway. There's something you need to see. Come around here, Mrs. Strickland."

Bobbie walked around her desk. In spite of his halfhearted resistance, Mrs. Brown pulled the back of DeShawn's shirt up. Bobbie clamped her lips shut to keep a gasp from escaping. His back was crosshatched with raised, maroon welts. Some were encrusted with dried blood. Bobbie had seen these kinds of marks before, knew they had been made with an ironing cord.

"Go get the nurse, Mrs. Brown."

"Don't get the nurse. I'm sorry. I'll be good," DeShawn pleaded.

Bobbie nodded to Mrs. Brown and she left.

"Who did this to you, DeShawn?"

"I can't tell. I'll get in trouble."

"No, you won't. Come here." Bobbie took his hand and led him to stand in front of her. She put her hand under his chin and raised his head. "You've got to tell me. I'll protect you."

Bobbie saw the tough exterior melt in the big tears that formed in his eyes. She pulled him to her and hugged him close. He made no sound, but she felt the wet spot on her shoulder where he laid his head. "This should not have happened. You're just a little boy. You didn't deserve this." Bobbie was careful not to press against his back. She knew she was breaking the rules. She wasn't supposed to touch the children. But sometimes the rules had to be broken, and she was willing to take the consequences. The scars on his back would heal. She wasn't sure the ones on his heart would. "Tell me who, baby."

He shook his head against her shoulder.

"If your mama did this, we can get her some help so it'll never happen again."

"Wasn't Mama," he mumbled. "Was James Earl."

"James Earl who? What's his last name?"

"I'un know. He's Mama's boyfriend. He stay with us. Sometime."

A shudder went through Bobbie. The door opened and the nurse stopped at the sight of the boy in Bobbie's embrace. She met Bobbie's eyes, then walked over. Without releasing DeShawn, Bobbie pulled the back of his shirt up. Mrs. Peoples's face hardened. Then she reached out for him.

"DeShawn, I want you to go with Mrs. Peoples to her office. She may have to take you to the hospital."

At that, DeShawn started bawling, "I want my mama! I want my mama!"

"Hush, baby. I'll call your mother. Does she know James Earl did this to you?"

"I want my mama! I want my mama!" His wailing continued as Mrs. Peoples took him down the hall.

Bobbie sat in her chair a long time, steeling herself for what she knew was coming. By lunch she had talked to a caseworker at Child Protective Services who said she was familiar with the family from previous referrals, a detective in the Child Abuse Unit, a doctor at the hospital, and DeShawn's mother—who had cussed her out. The last call was to Scott Douglas, the school district's lawyer. That he was almost gleeful about it saddened her. For him, this was a turn for the better in the potential lawsuit. Bobbie couldn't find anything gleeful or better about it. But she couldn't be angry with him; he was just looking out for the school. Sitting up there in a tall building downtown, he would never close his eyes and see crosshatched welts on a little boy's back.

At lunchtime, Bobbie patrolled the cafeteria. Over the sea of heads, she wondered how many of these children needed hugs. And whether there was anything she could do to save them. How had she missed the signs in DeShawn? He wasn't really a bad kid. She remembered the time he'd given a boy a black eye and a fat lip. She'd had to write that in his record. But she'd also mentioned that he'd jumped the boy in defense of one of the girls. None of them were bad kids. They were just kids dealing with the cards life had dealt them. Had she become so inured to the violence and chaos in her school over the years that she'd forgotten that? Had rigid adherence to the rules edged out her compassion?

Back in her office, still questioning herself, she pulled the evaluations from her briefcase and reviewed them. She made minor changes to a couple of them but was otherwise satisfied. When she got to Bill Gibson's, she drummed her pen on the desk a long time. She wanted to do the right thing. But what was the right thing? Maybe theirs was just a personality conflict. Perhaps he wouldn't fight another principal, wouldn't undermine his or her authority. Perhaps he would work better with a male principal. But if it was just in his nature to be a backstabbing SOB, she would be visiting misery on a colleague. And she'd be sure to hear about it in the Circle of Principals meetings for the entire year. On the other hand, the meetings were only monthly, and that was better than having to deal with Bill every single day.

*　　*　　*

The lights from inside the house shone through the glass walls and were sufficient for them to see what they were doing.

"You remember how we did this before? Let me bear the weight. You just guide it. Watch your toes too," Ray said as he pulled the cabinet onto the bed of the truck.

When the cabinet was positioned on the dolly, Ray put his small toolbox inside it and set a thick quilt on top. Inside the house, he rolled the dolly over to the stairwell.

"I wish you had let me bring Jimbo. He can really put away some beer, but to be as skinny as he is, that ol' boy is surprisingly strong. It's going to be tricky, getting this thing upstairs. He and I could have done it faster. Just carried it up. But this will work too," Ray said, spreading the quilt on the floor at the foot of the stairs. He eased the cabinet onto the quilt.

"Now, you get on the front side, up two steps. All I want you to do is pull on the quilt hard enough to keep it taut. Don't try to pull the weight of the cabinet. I'll push from the bottom."

"Okay. I can do that."

Once they got the cabinet to the second floor, Ray pulled it into the master bathroom and set about attaching it to the wall, while Bobbie stood in the doorway. From his back on the floor, he called, "Why don't you bring up something from the cooler."

Bobbie came back with a couple of beers and set one on the floor near him. She leaned against the doorjamb, watching him work. Despite his exertion getting the cabinet upstairs, his T-shirt was still tucked neatly in his cargo shorts. She liked the way the muscles in his arms and abdomen tightened when he used the screwdriver. And his thighs . . . Bobbie realized she was entertaining unholy thoughts, so she left the room.

She made a circle, wandering around the top floor of the house, pretending that she lived there—with Ray. And Monee, of course. She even picked out Monee's room, the one at the far end of the hallway. She could imagine Monee lounging on the velvet-padded window seat, reading a book. Back in the bedroom she would share with Ray, Bobbie opened the French doors and stepped out onto the deck.

Standing at the rail, she could see the lake. Lights on the other side cast reflections across its surface. She wondered what kind of jobs those people had—and where she had been when they were being passed out. Probably inheritances and trust funds, she decided. These kinds of houses didn't come with just hard work and effort. She thought about some of the kids' mothers at her school. A lot of them worked two jobs and still didn't have basics such as a car or health insurance. The sound of the door opening behind her broke her reverie.

"Whatcha thinking about?" Ray asked, joining her at the railing. He shook the quilt out and let it fall to the deck.

"Nothing."

"Nothing? A beautiful sight like this and you're thinking about nothing?"

A sudden rustling in the branches of the tree next to the deck startled Bobbie and she jumped back away from the railing.

"It's just an old owl," Ray said. "I've seen him before when I was here. Come on, sit down."

Bobbie kicked her shoes off and sat cross-legged on the quilt.

"So tell me what you were thinking about."

"Well, actually, I was thinking how unfair life is. How some people work so hard and have nothing. Always only one paycheck from the po'house. Others don't have to hit a lick at a snake, and they can live like this. And the whole thing just perpetuates itself. Most of the kids at my school haven't even seen a house like this—except on television. Let me stop thinking about this before I get mad." She blew out an angry breath, then inhaled deeply, sat up straight, and put a smile on her face.

"Doesn't look like much has been done since the last time I was here," she said. "And that was a while ago."

"No, hardly anything. A couple of weeks ago, I talked to the fella it belongs to. Young guy. He moved here from California last year to work for one of these dot-com companies. His company took a nosedive along with the rest of them. Now he's debating whether to finish the house."

"So what'll happen to the house?"

"I don't know. You want it?"

"Boy, shut up." She laughed. "You know I couldn't even think about a house like this."

"I know for a fact that you could get a good deal on it, if you'll take it 'as is.' Doesn't have toilets. Would that be a problem for you?"

Bobbie puffed out a little laugh. "You're so crazy."

Ray took her hand and raised it to his lips. "I'm crazy about you." He planted a little kiss on her lips. "Are you crazy about me too?"

Bobbie gave him a teasing smile. "I'm not sure."

"Well, let me see what I can do to bring a little certainty to this situation." He kissed her again, and this one was meant to be convincing.

"Just a little bit crazy about me yet?"

Bobbie shook her head. "Not yet," she said, joining his teasing game.

"You just want me to kiss you again." So he did, easing her back on the quilt.

Bobbie liked the solid feel of his weight on her. She put her arms around his neck, inviting him to go further. And he did, nuzzling her neck, then the swell of her breast. Ray leaned on his side and propped himself up on one elbow. With his other hand, he released the buttons on her blouse, one at a time. Bobbie felt the warm night breeze brush across her bared skin.

"Maybe we shouldn't be carrying on like this out in public," she said.

"Nobody out here but the owl. I want you to tell him that you're crazy about me."

Bobbie stuck out her bottom lip and shook her head.

Ray stroked her thigh, palming her soft flesh. Then his hand wandered inside the leg of her shorts. Bobbie knew this was getting serious. She thought of all the reasons why she should stop him. But none of them were as compelling as the warmth of his hand.

"Tell him," Ray urged in a coarse whisper.

His breath was warm and moist against her ear, and with each stroke of his hand, sweet chills snaked down her spine. She wanted nothing more than to envelope him in her softness. But she also wanted to prolong and savor each moment of what she already knew would be their first time together. To keep him from knowing that, she slowly shook her head.

"We'll see about that." Then he touched her in a place that tested her resolve. The third time he did it, her body betrayed her and told him what she had refused to.

Ray looked down into her face and smiled. Then he kissed her slowly, and sweetly, and deeply. Before the long kiss was over, he had shed his clothing and relieved her of the rest of hers. Slowly, he entered her and, with each deepening stroke, urged her again, "Tell him." Bobbie still refused. He turned on his back, pulling her on top of him, caressing the length of her body with a slow hand. Then he went still, and waited. Bobbie tried to outwait him, but the fullness in her wouldn't let her. Ray clasped the back of her knees and pulled them forward until she rested on her shins. He slowly rocked her back and forth, sending waves of pleasure through her, until she took the movement over herself. Then he let her have her way.

Bobbie's surrender was total and complete. And the owl heard it.

22

On the way back to her house, Bobbie was infused with the afterglow of their lovemaking. Every now and then, Ray would reach over and entwine his fingers in hers, then bring her hand to his lips. But a hundred questions nagged at her. Now what? Had she been too hasty and free? Would she regret what she'd done in the morning? Was this a deal where, now, Ray would pull a disappearing act?

When he turned on her street, Bobbie could see a car parked in front of her house. She hoped like anything that the baby-sitter didn't have a boy over. She had used Lisa several times to baby-sit Monee. She attended Mt. Moriah and lived on the next street. She was fifteen, acted responsibly, and didn't have a car. Bobbie liked that. Once they got cars, they got real jobs and weren't available to baby-sit. But if Lisa had a boy over, Bobbie would be in a spot. She couldn't keep that information from Lisa's mother, and then Lisa probably wouldn't want to sit for her again.

"What's Sonny doing here?" Ray asked, almost to himself. "I guess he's looking for me."

Bobbie didn't answer, but she had a bad feeling about Sonny being at her house. Since the argument, she had assiduously avoided any mention of him to Ray. And Ray hadn't brought him up either. They had both ignored the elephant in the room. It looked as if their truce was about to be tested.

On the porch, she used her key to open the door. In the living room, Bobbie tightened her lips at what she saw. Darlene and Monee sat on the floor. Sonny was on the couch, a high-ball glass on the coffee table in front of him.

"Hi, Mama. I wasn't expecting you back so soon," Darlene said.

"I guess not" was the calmest thing Bobbie could think of to say. If it had just been the two of them, she would have given Darlene three pieces of her mind. But she couldn't act like that in front of Ray and his son, or in front of Monee.

"Where's Lisa?" Bobbie asked.

"We took her home. She said you could pay her at church on Sunday," Darlene said.

"Granny, we went and got some ice cream too," Monee said, beaming.

Bobbie forced a smile. "That's nice, Monee. It's past your bedtime. You go ahead and get ready."

"Aw, Granny, it's Friday. And it's only eleven-thirty. I don't have school tomorrow."

"Did you hear what I said?" Bobbie said, more sternly than she'd intended.

Monee reluctantly rose. She hugged Darlene's neck, then walked past Bobbie. Her footfalls on the stairs were more pronounced than necessary. Bobbie decided she'd deal with Monee's behavior in the morning. Right now she had to deal with Darlene.

"Can I see you out on the porch for a minute?"

Bobbie pulled the door closed behind them.

"What are you doing in my house?"

Darlene looked chastised. "I thought it would be okay."

"Why?"

"The judge said I could see her every other Friday. This is Friday."

"Yeah, well, that little stunt you pulled last time made that null and void. I'm sure if the judge knew about that, she would change her mind."

"I didn't take her away, Mama. We've just been sitting here most of the time. I'm trying to prove myself."

"And why are you with Sonny?"

"I like him, Mama. He's nice to me."

"You shouldn't like him too much. He's married, Darlene."

"Separated."

"Well, whatever. It's time for you to go."

Darlene turned and went back in the house. Bobbie followed her in. She noticed that Darlene still wore Mrs. Swink's ruby ring. That was a good sign. Bobbie had expected it would be long gone by now.

In the living room, the men were engaged in quiet, but strained, conversation.

"Come on, Sonny. We'd better go," Darlene said, picking up her purse.

★ ★ ★

Saturday evening, Bobbie stood at the sink, washing vegetables for dinner. Ray sat at the kitchen table, concentrating on a diagram in his *Fine Furniture* magazine.

"Did you ever find those tools you were looking for?" she asked.

Ray shook his head. "I know they've got to be around somewhere. But I've looked everywhere. And the funny thing is, now I can't find my little jambox that I keep in the shop. Maybe it's in the motor home. But I don't remember putting it in there. I'm just getting where I forget everything."

Bobbie didn't want to revisit their argument, but it had been on her mind, and she just had to say it.

"Is Sonny still here?"

"Yeah, why?" he asked, looking up from the magazine.

It wasn't too late to turn around. She could just shrug it off and change the subject. But Bobbie knew he wouldn't let her.

"Several of your things have come up missing since he came."

"What are you trying to say?"

"I think you should check the pawnshops."

Ray looked confused. "Pawnshops?"

"He's hanging out with Darlene."

"I intended to talk to Sonny about that when he got home, except I was asleep by the time he got in. He's a married man, and he shouldn't be cavorting around with another woman as though he isn't. But what do pawnshops have to do with it?"

Bobbie hesitated, then charged on. "Birds of a feather, you know."

Ray didn't answer for a long minute. Slowly, he closed the magazine. He could feel himself being drawn into the argument. But he couldn't just let her keep picking at Sonny.

"Just because your child has drug problems doesn't mean everybody's does."

"You're the one with missing tools," she shot back.

"I raised Sonny right."

"Are you suggesting that I didn't raise Darlene right?"

"I'm not suggesting anything. I'm taking up for my son. You just don't like him. First you insinuate that he's a drunk. Now you're making him out to be a drug addict. You need to focus on your own child."

Bobbie had a mouthful of smart for him, but she kept it in. She didn't need to defend herself.

"I was just trying to help. I've been through this, Ray. I recognize the signs."

Ray stood and tucked the magazine under his arm.

"I think I'd better go. I'll call you tomorrow. Maybe you'll have a different perspective."

Ray stood at the kitchen counter, drinking a beer. All the way home, he'd turned the conversation over in his mind. The more he thought about it, the madder he'd become. He didn't care what she said, his child was not a drug addict. And he wasn't a drunk either. His child wouldn't steal from him. He'd been a strong father. He'd worked hard to see that his boys had everything they needed. He'd given them both a good education. He had to admit, though, that he was a little concerned that Sonny hadn't made up with Myrna and gone home. Some other things worried him as well. For one, the hours he kept. It was almost as if Sonny was avoiding him.

Ray felt ashamed of himself, but he went in Sonny's room and turned on the light. He stood there a long time just looking around, trying to persuade himself that he was just doing it to prove Bobbie wrong. He looked through the paraphernalia strewn on the dresser—coins, little notes with phone numbers on them. Just the kinds of things a man would empty his pockets of. But even if Sonny had stolen Ray's things and pawned them, surely he wouldn't leave a pawn slip out on the dresser where it could be easily spotted. Once Ray accepted that he was looking, he thought he might as well be thorough. That way, he would be even more convinced that he was right.

Sonny's suitcase was on the chair. Ray walked over to it and stood with his arms folded across his chest. Then he unzipped it. Clothes were jumbled inside, not neatly folded as Ray had taught him. He sifted through the clothes and found a thick manila envelope. He pulled it out and opened it. Inside, he found divorce papers and a restraining order. They were dated five months ago. He wondered why Sonny hadn't told him the whole story. He replaced the envelope under the clothes and ran his hand in one of the compartments. The cardboard receipt that he pulled out had a seven-digit number printed in red, just above "Best Pawn, Inc." and the address. On the back was printed, "We pay top prices—24 hours a day."

From inside the truck, Ray saw the sign that read, "Doors locked at 10 P.M. Use walk-up window." He looked at his watch. It was after midnight, but you couldn't tell by the line in front of the pawnshop. He drove away.

The next morning, Ray was back, parked in the same space. He went straight to where the hand tools were. A drill just like his had a $60 price tag. The electric hammer was priced at $100. Neither was his, and he was relieved. When he presented the pawn ticket, the clerk excused himself a moment, then returned and laid his drill and electric hammer on the counter. "That'll be forty dollars with the interest and all. You came just in time. One more day and they would have been released to the floor."

Ray took out his checkbook. He had paid more than that for the drill when it was new. He always bought top-of-the-line tools. Ray stopped writing the check.

"Uh, you know, I have some other things here. But I left the tickets at home. Can I get them too while I'm here?"

"What's your name?"

"Sonny Caldwell."

The clerk typed into the computer. "I don't show a Sonny Caldwell."

"Oh, sorry. Raymond Caldwell Jr."

The clerk typed that in. "Let's see. A jambox, a small compressor, and a power painter. Would that be it?"

Ray gripped the steering wheel so hard, his hands hurt. But that was nothing compared to how they were going to hurt when he got through kicking Sonny's ass. He drove straight to his house, but Sonny's car wasn't there. He backed out of the driveway and drove to Bobbie's house. He sat in the truck awhile, breathing deep and gathering his thoughts.

When she opened the door, the look on her face told him this was going to be harder than he'd expected.

"We need to talk."

"Talk."

He could hear the television and knew Monee was in the living room within earshot. "Could you come outside?"

Bobbie didn't answer, but she stepped out on the porch. She folded her arms across her chest and gave him a questioning look.

"I found my tools."

"Good. I'm glad for you."

"You were right. They were in the pawnshop." He looked down as he said it.

Bobbie didn't say anything.

Ray looked back up at her. "I'm sorry for what I said. I just didn't know. I couldn't believe it."

"Okay." Her arms were still folded across her chest.

"I'm trying to apologize. Can't you accept that?"

"Okay. I accept your apology. I'm glad you found your tools. Now, if you'll excuse me, I'm busy."

For a long time, Ray stared at the door she'd closed in his face. He felt like kicking it down. Didn't she see what he was going through?

Bobbie leaned back against the door, her eyes closed. What had she just done? Lost the best man she'd ever had? Why was she being cruel to him? It wasn't like her. She had seen the pain in his eyes. She wanted to fling the door open, run to him, and put her arms around him. But she couldn't make herself do it.

⋆　　⋆　　⋆

Sonny had been out all night and still hadn't come home. Ray had taken the compressor back to his workshop, but he put the drill, electric hammer, and power painter on the coffee table. The $250 check he'd written hadn't hurt him, it was that he'd had to write it that stung. He sat in his recliner determined to stay there until Sonny came in. He hadn't decided whether he was going to knock the hell out of him first, then talk to him, or vice versa. He almost grabbed a beer from the refrigerator, but took an orange juice instead. He wanted to be stone-cold sober when Sonny got there.

Finally he picked up the phone and called her.

As soon as Bobbie put the car in park, Monee hopped out. By the time Bobbie got to Mrs. Swink's room, Monee was already there.

"We came by to see if you needed anything. We're going to the grocery store." Bobbie was so pleased with Mrs. Swink's progress. Most days she didn't show any signs of confusion, and her attitude had improved considerably. In fact, lately she had been downright cheerful. But not today.

"Sit down, Bobbie. I don't need anything from the store, but I sure would like a nice, cold soft drink. Could Monee get it for me?"

"Sure!" Monee said.

"Get my purse off the dresser."

When Monee returned with the purse, Mrs. Swink handed her a dollar bill. "There are several machines around. But the one with the coldest drinks is on the third floor. Can you take the elevator by yourself?"

"I sure can."

"When you get off, go down the long hallway, turn right, and it's at the end of another long hallway. You won't get lost now, will you?"

"No, ma'am." Monee's eyes shone with the anticipation of doing a grown-up task.

As soon as she'd closed the door, Mrs. Swink turned to Bobbie. "Something's wrong, Bobbie. What is it?"

"Nothing. Everything's fine." Bobbie wouldn't look her in the eye.

"You can't fool me. I've known you too long. It's got something to do with your new fellow. Since he came on the scene, you've been happier than I've ever seen you. Now your mouth is turned down. What happened?"

Bobbie told her.

"So you were right. And he acknowledged that. What more do you want from the man?"

"I don't know."

"What are you going to do?"

"Nothing."

"Well, you'll just be a silly goose. A prideful silly goose. The man said he was sorry. If you nurse that hurt, it'll just fester and grow. Seems like to me you have a chance to have some happiness in your life. You've worked hard, Bobbie. Done your duty. Even by Monee. And you've had to do it alone. Now you have a chance to have somebody decent in your life. Don't throw that away. If you do, you're going to end up alone."

"I've got Monee," Bobbie said defensively.

"Yes, you have Monee now. But she's going to grow up and leave you, Bobbie. That's the way it's supposed to be.

And it'll come quicker than you know. The years pass fast. You'll get to the end of your life and you will have missed years of happiness. Just like me. I nursed the pain of my Zeke and Mandy. I blamed God and everybody else. I closed myself off from everybody and from life. Now I have just a few years left. But I plan to make the most of them. I'm gonna cram as much in them as I can. Don't make the mistake I did. Accept his apology and move on. We all make mistakes. That's what makes us human. You see all these old people around here? There's not one of them who wouldn't trade places with you. To have your health. And to have a chance to share their life with someone. To not be alone."

Before Bobbie could answer, the door opened and Monee came in. "Mrs. Swink, did you know there's a swimming pool on the third floor? And a gym?"

"The pool is not on the way to the soft drink machine," Mrs. Swink said with a twinkle in her eye.

Monee looked sheepish. "I got lost."

"No, you didn't. You were exploring. That's okay."

A big smile came to Monee's face.

"Y'all go on to the store now. Get some peaches. I want a cobbler. The food here isn't as bad as Raf made out, but I sure have a taste for your peach cobbler, Bobbie. And I want homemade crust too. No shortcuts."

Bobbie noted that Raf had been coming up in Mrs. Swink's conversation a lot lately. Bobbie stood. "I'll see. Come on, Monee."

"Here, honey. Take this drink. I lost my taste for it." Mrs. Swink handed the can to Monee. "And go in the bedroom and get Mandy. I'm feeling a lot better these days. You can take her home with you now."

At the door, Mrs. Swink held Bobbie back. "You think about what I said." She waited a minute, then added, "And bring enough cobbler for Raf. I've been bragging on your cooking to him."

23

THE SMELL of cinnamon hung heavy in Bobbie's kitchen. Three baking dishes of steaming peach cobbler were on the stove. Bobbie could tell these were some of the best ones she'd ever made. She'd doubled her recipe, then divided it into three dishes—one for Mrs. Swink, one for her and Monee, and one for Ray. Bobbie carefully smoothed a sheet of tinfoil around the edges of one hot glass dish. She wrapped pot holders around the handles and carried it to her car.

Monee didn't want to come with her. She was engrossed in the movie Bobbie had rented for her. Maybe she was getting old enough to stay by herself. Still, Bobbie wasn't comfortable about it. It was dark outside and threatening to rain. She didn't plan to stay. She would just surprise him, drop off the cobbler, then come right back. He didn't live that far away. This would be a little test to see if Monee was ready.

Bobbie drove slowly to make sure the cobbler didn't spill.

When she reached his house, a car she didn't recognize was parked next to his truck in the driveway. Maybe she shouldn't stop. She should have called first. Well, she hadn't planned to stay. Just drop the dish off. She pulled the car to the curb and turned off the motor. The night was quiet, except for the occasional rumble of thunder. From the sound, she thought she could make it back home before the rain came.

When she got to the door, she had to ring the bell with her elbow. No one came. She rang it again. Then she heard voices coming from the back of the house, so she walked on the cobblestone pathway around the side of the house. The workshop was brightly lit. She could see Ray through the window. And the woman too.

Bobbie stopped in her tracks. She couldn't see the woman very well from where she stood, but she could tell she was petite and had long hair. She and Ray were standing close together, facing each other. She couldn't make out what they were saying, or the tone of their voices, but she could see the woman as she raised her arms and put them around Ray's neck. He wrapped his arms around her, pulled her tightly against him, and buried his face in her shoulders. The woman's hands rubbed up and down his back.

Bobbie closed her mouth, then tightened her lips. She blinked when a raindrop fell on her eyelash. Then another hit her cheek. She looked down at the dish in her hands when she felt the heat from the dish seeping through the padded cloth. The rain fell in earnest now. She felt drops tingle her scalp, then run down the back of her neck. She blinked her eyes but didn't know if it was from the rain or from her tears. She felt the urge to throw the dish through the workshop window. That would break up this little party.

But that would put her in the role of a crazy woman and thrust the other woman into the role of the victim. Her beef wasn't with the woman. Her beef was with a lying, no-count man. He was just like the rest of them.

Bobbie turned and hurried to her car. She resisted the urge to burn rubber getting away. She didn't want him to know she'd been there.

As she drove, Bobbie fumbled around for the package of tissues she kept in the car, but couldn't find it in the dark. So she wiped her eyes with the back of her hand. At the stoplight, she gave in to it. All of the tears that she'd held back for so long poured out of her. A salty taste filled the back of her throat. When she turned on the interior light, she found the tissues and blew her nose. Then she cried some more. She felt like screaming, so she did. Then she put her forehead on the steering wheel and let the tears fall freely in her lap. She could have stayed there for an hour, but the blast of a horn from the car that pulled up behind made her snap to.

The next morning, Bobbie gathered up the gimme cap and two T-shirts that Ray had left at her house back when he was building the cabinets for her and put them in a sack. She wanted to put the jewelry box he had made for Monee in too, but it wasn't hers to return. After she dropped Monee off at school, she drove straight to his house. She dropped the sack on his doorstep and turned to leave. But it wasn't enough. He had to know how he'd hurt her. He needed to know what a low-down SOB she thought he was. Not only had he taken a part of her that couldn't be returned, he'd conned Monee. Bobbie turned around and rang the bell.

When the door opened, Ray stood there in a maroon velour robe with a look of surprise on his face.

"Morning. I wasn't expecting you. No school today?"

"Yes, there's school today. I'm on my way. I brought your stuff. I've got something to ask you."

"Well, come on in," he said, stepping back from the door. Bobbie stepped inside.

"Do you have time for a cup of coffee?"

"No. This won't take but a minute. Here's your stuff," she said, thrusting the sack at him. "I just want you to know—"

"Ray, where is the toothpaste?" a woman's voice called from down the hallway.

They looked at each other. Bobbie's eyes narrowed into slits. Ray looked trapped. He opened his mouth, then closed it. Bobbie crimped hers.

The woman she'd seen last night appeared in the hall doorway, wearing a tangerine kimono with a seductive slit up one side.

"Ray, didn't you hear me? Oh." She pulled the kimono tighter around her and ran her hand through her tousled hair.

There was a long, awkward silence while each of them waited for the other to break it. Bobbie and the woman sized each other up.

Ray cleared his throat. "Uh, Bobbie, this is my wife—I mean my ex—I mean Loretta."

Bobbie wasn't sure what the proper etiquette would be for this kind of situation, so she just nodded her head in acknowledgment.

Loretta walked over to her and held out her hand. "It's good to meet you."

Bobbie half-turned to the front door.

"Wait," Ray said.

Bobbie turned back and stared at Ray, her eyes almost in a squint, her jaws tight. At that moment, she wanted nothing more than to leave this house and forget she had ever met him.

"I understand that you are the reason that I'm here," Loretta said, dropping her hand.

Bobbie's eyebrows raised in a pregnant question mark.

"Why don't you sit down. I'll get us some coffee," Loretta said. With self-possessed steps, she headed for the kitchen.

When Loretta came back with a tray, Bobbie and Ray were sitting on opposite ends of the couch. Bobbie quickly averted her eyes so that Loretta couldn't see the evil, sidelong squint she had focused on Ray. He looked as if he had a lot to say but didn't know where to start. Loretta set the tray on the coffee table. She handed a mug to Ray with the confidence of years of practice that she knew how he took his coffee.

"How do you take yours?" she asked Bobbie.

"Black." Bobbie struggled to maintain her composure.

Loretta handed her a mug, took her own, and sat in the armchair across from them. She crossed one shapely leg over the other. She took a testing sip from her mug, then set it on the lamp table beside the chair. She looked directly at Bobbie.

"I want to thank you."

"Thank me? For what?" Bobbie asked, caught off guard.

"For helping him to see," she said, nodding at Ray.

Bobbie looked to Ray, confused. Ray looked down at his lap, so Bobbie looked back at Loretta.

"Ray refused to see it, but Sonny has had a problem for a while. Now he's lost his job. Myrna—his wife—finally gave up on him. Of course, as a mother, I will never give up on him. But he can't come to my house. Even if I would allow it, my new husband won't. I'm almost ashamed to say it, but that's the way it is. That's why he's here in Austin instead of Kansas City with us. You must think I'm a terrible person." Her tone suggested that she didn't really care what Bobbie thought.

"It's not my place to judge," Bobbie said. "I'm sure you're doing what you think is best." Although she was still wary of Loretta, she liked the sound of "new husband" a lot, and she felt like a hypocrite for not telling Loretta just how much she understood. But this wasn't the time or place for true confessions.

Loretta leaned forward with her elbows on the arms of the chair, her fingers interwoven and resting on her knee. She spoke directly to Bobbie.

"Let me tell you, honey. I've been up and down with that boy so many times, I'm just not going through it again. I barely got him out of high school. And five years of college was just as much of a struggle. It wasn't easy bearing all that weight by myself—"

"Wait just a minute, Loretta," Ray interrupted. "You make it sound like—"

Loretta continued talking to Bobbie. "Oh, Ray was a good daddy. I wouldn't try to take that away from him. He provided for us very well. But he was busy. He was an officer. It's critical to an officer's career that his family toe the line. We were as much in the military as he was. We just didn't get a paycheck. Things are different in the new military. But I was in the old military and I was a lieutenant colonel's wife. It was my job to keep everything wrapped up nice and neat in a pretty package so the officer could concentrate on his duties. I did that," she said matter-of-factly. "When I retired—"

"When *you* retired?" Ray's whole countenance was indignant.

"Yes, when I retired," Loretta said, emphasizing every word. She turned back to Bobbie. "I'd had enough. That boy has nearly driven me crazy. The counselor I went to told me that Sonny would have to hit rock bottom, and that I was interfering with that. So I stopped. Poor little Myrna hung as long as she could, but she finally filed for divorce. I stay in touch with her because she has my grandchild. Anyway, from what Ray told me, it sounds like the bottom has come. I don't believe he would have seen it, if it hadn't been for you. He's always had a mote in his eye for that boy. He'd have been out there in his shop, putting all his little nails and screws in order according to size and refusing to believe what's right in front of his face. He wouldn't listen to me. He was so angry about the divorce—and having to split *our* retirement." Loretta cast an affirming glance at Ray, then looked back at Bobbie. "When Michael and I married—"

"That's enough, Loretta," Ray snapped, rising from the couch. "We need to get back to the business at hand."

Loretta rolled her eyes at him, but she stopped talking and sat back in the chair.

Ray began pacing as he explained to Bobbie, "I called Loretta after I left your house the other night. She flew in yesterday. We've agreed to work together on this. Except we really don't know what to do now. She told me about this intervention thing. We were going to confront him, but Sonny hasn't been here since she came. And he hasn't been at Mama's. Do you have any idea what we can do? We can't just keep sitting here waiting."

"Well, Ray, I obviously don't—"

"But you seem to kind of know, you know, ah, know your way around the city. Maybe we could go find him."

Loretta stood up and stretched. "That's better than any idea *I've* come up with. I'll throw on some clothes. We can all go."

"Well, if you want to go looking for him, I do know some places to try. But some of these places are kind of rough," Bobbie warned as Loretta walked away.

"Then Ray had better bring his gun," Loretta called over her shoulder from the hallway.

"No, don't do that," Bobbie said quickly to Ray. "Some-body might get hurt."

Ray cupped his hands around Bobbie's shoulders and looked in her eyes.

"Thank you." He planted a soft kiss on her forehead, then hugged her to him.

"You go get dressed," Bobbie said. "I need to call my school and let them know I may not be in today."

Later that night, Ray and Bobbie sat relaxing on Bobbie's porch swing.

"That cobbler was delicious. Best I ever had. Can I take the rest of it home with me?"

Bobbie nodded her head. "I brought it to you last night, but you were all hugged up with another woman."

Ray smiled and kissed her on the tip of her nose. "I really appreciate what you did today. I couldn't believe I had to wrestle with that boy like that. My own son. A little more, and I'd have punched his damn lights out. I'm still mad about my tools. I hope they can help him in that hospital."

"Shoal Creek is good—if you have the money. Sonny is lucky. Most of them have to get in trouble with the law to get any help. And what help there is still isn't much." Bobbie slowly shook her head. "Did Loretta get off okay?"

"Yes. She called from the airport. Said to tell you thank you and that she'd be in touch with you." Ray cast a sidelong glance at Bobbie. "I don't know whether I like that."

They swung back and forth. The night was quiet. The street was dark.

"Bobbie, can I ask you something?"

She nodded.

"Are you still crazy about me?"

"Who said I was ever crazy about you?"

"That ol' owl said you were crazy about me."

"Humph. Shows you what owls know."

In the dark, Ray smiled. He kept the swing moving at a leisurely pace. He loved being here. He loved having her company. In fact, he thought he might just love her.

"Why didn't you tell me that your neighbor moved back home?"

"Who?"

"Mrs. Swink. I thought she was selling the house. Did she bring the old Italian dude you told me about with her?"

"What are you talking about?" Bobbie asked, sitting up a little.

"There are lights on down there at her house. She didn't move home?"

They were both out of the swing at the same time and headed down the street. When they got to the house, they slowed their pace and became cautious. Ray told Bobbie to wait in the yard by the FOR SALE sign. He crept up on the porch. Bobbie wouldn't wait this time. She eased up behind him and peered over his shoulder. Through the open window they could see Darlene, but they couldn't see whom she was talking to.

"I swear, it was here. Right here," Darlene said.

"Well, it ain't there now." It was a man's voice, heavy with threat.

"She put them in this big Bible that she keeps on this shelf. That Bible's been there as long as I can remember."

"So where is it now?"

"I don't know. I've looked everywhere."

"You 'bout a lying bitch. I guess I'm just gonna have to beat the truth outta you. You know I could beat you to death. Some Realtor will find your body. In fact, that would settle it all."

"What do you mean?"

"You say the old lady doesn't know what's in the envelope you put in her Bible. Maybe the old lady's got the Bible with her. Where is she?"

Darlene's eyes widened at the threat, then narrowed. "Like I would tell you."

"Oh, you'll tell me. Before I'd let you make my mama a laughingstock in this rinky-dink town, I'll take your head off. You know, I really used to think I was in love with you. And all the time, it turns out, you were sexing my daddy up.

Was I a fool or what? But I'ma straighten all this mess out. I'll get the negatives and my grama's locket from her, and you keep yo' damn mouth shut. All you got to do is tell me where the old lady is."

Darlene shook her head. "You leave her out of this. I've got to go." She started walking toward the door. Trey tackled her, then punched her in the face three times before Ray burst through the door, grabbed Trey around his neck, and dragged him off Darlene. Bobbie rushed to Darlene's side, shielding her with her body.

Ray's grip around Trey's neck was tight enough to cut his wind off. Trey's eyes bulged, then he elbowed Ray in the stomach to break his hold. The blow took Ray by surprise, and by the time he recovered, Trey was in a fighting crouch, rolling his fists around, ready to attack.

Ray began to weave, watching Trey's eyes and taunting him. "Come on, son. Just come on. I've been spoiling for a fight all day. I already whupped a boy your size. And that was for breakfast. It's suppertime now. Come on." Trey charged at him, but Ray slipped aside. Trey stumbled into the desk, but pushed off, turned around, and readied for another charge.

Ray backed across the room, away from the women on the floor. He held up one fist and beckoned with his other hand. "Come on over here. Get some of this. You think you bad. Come on. You know, I've always thought that a man who'd hit a woman ain't shit. A punk. Come on, get some of this, you little mama's boy."

Trey charged at him again, growling. At the last nanosecond, Ray stepped aside. Trey butted his head into the wall, bounced back, and fell on his back, groaning.

Ray stood over him. "Not only are you a punk, you're a dumb-ass punk." Before Ray knew what happened, Trey grabbed his ankle and jerked him off-balance. As they wrestled around on the floor, Trey's youth gave him an advantage. But it couldn't overcome years of training, so Ray ended up on top. He threw a punch that he intended to be jaw-breaking and was drawing back for another.

Just then, three policemen charged into the house, shouting, "Freeze! Freeze! Everybody freeze!"

24

BEDLAM REIGNED in Mrs. Swink's living room. Ray thought he was being attacked by Trey's backup, and he put up a furious resistance when he felt himself being dragged off him. It took two of the officers to gain control of him. He got a solid punch to one's stomach before they subdued him. Trey shot to his feet and started after Ray, but the sight of the third officer's drawn gun chilled him out.

Once the combatants were separated and handcuffed, it took a little while for the police to sort it out. From the injuries to Darlene's face, it was obvious that one of them had assaulted her and the other was defending her. It just wasn't clear who. Trey claimed that he was defending Darlene from Ray. Darlene was too beat down and scared to speak up through her busted lip. She held on to Bobbie as tight as she could, with her face buried in Bobbie's chest, and refused an ambulance. Bobbie told them the truth, but she hadn't brought any ID with her. Only when Mrs.

Downs from next door hobbled in on her cane and told them that she was the one who had called for the police when she saw Trey dragging Darlene up the steps to the unoccupied house did they release the cuffs on Ray's hands. By that time, Idalia had appeared on the porch. As soon as she got the story from Mrs. Downs, she went to take charge of Monee. The officer who had been hit in the stomach was still a little huffy, but the sergeant assured Ray that no charges would be filed against him.

As they struggled to bring Trey to the patrol car, he was shouting, "I'ma kill you, bitch. You just wait."

When the trio returned from the emergency room, Ray stopped the truck at Idalia's to pick Monee up. Since it was 3 A.M., Idalia suggested they let Monee stay until morning instead of waking her now. Ray knew that the women needed some time alone, so he saw them to Bobbie's door, gave her a kiss on the forehead, and left.

The house was quiet. Darlene and Bobbie sat on the couch, so close together that their hips were touching. Darlene's head rested on Bobbie's shoulder and Bobbie's arm was around Darlene's shoulder. Bobbie could remember them sitting this way before, but it had been a very long time ago.

"Darlene, you've got to tell me what this is all about. It isn't over. There may be a trial. Whatever it is, I can handle it. Just tell me. Maybe I can help. What is it about Mrs. Swink's Bible? She doesn't have it. I have it."

Darlene didn't say anything for a long time. Finally she said, "Where is it?"

Bobbie took her arm from around Darlene and went to her car. She had put the Bible there to take to Mrs. Swink the day after she'd taken it from the house. But Mrs. Swink hadn't asked for it again and Bobbie had forgotten about it. She returned with the big tome, laid it in Darlene's lap, and sat next to her.

Darlene held on to the book with both hands as she told Bobbie everything, starting with the first time the preacher had come on to her. She told her of falling in love with this important and grown man. She told her of his promises to leave his wife, in order to keep her quiet about the baby. At first Bobbie was disbelieving, but the more Darlene told, the more she believed it. Finally, Darlene pulled a delicate chain with a little key from around her neck. She fitted the key in the lock on the Bible and opened it. On the first page there was elaborate cursive writing: *This Bible belongs to Suzie A. Swink. Do Not Bother.*

Darlene turned a half inch of pages, then turned two or three at a time until she reached the place she wanted. A neat, square hole was cut through two inches deep. Then she took out the envelope and handed it to Bobbie.

"This is what Trey was after. You can open it."

Darlene waited while Bobbie slid her finger under the flap of the envelope and broke the dried glue's hold. Bobbie took the pictures out and blinked a couple of times when she recognized Darlene and Marlon. They both looked so much younger. She saw the San Antonio Hilton logo in the background. She couldn't remember any church trip to San Antonio back then.

"He had found the copies of the pictures that I gave his daddy. Then he came after me, threatening and accusing.

Then he tore the pictures up and threw the pieces in my face. I should have kept my mouth shut, but after he'd called me all those bad names, I didn't want him to think he had got the best of me. So I told him I had the originals in a safe place. He thought if he could get them away from me, his mama couldn't find out. That even if I told, no one would believe me, and I would have nothing to back up my story."

Bobbie turned the envelope over and the locket fell out into her palm. She gave Darlene a questioning look.

"The locket belonged to Marlon's mother. He gave it to me way back then. It was supposed to be a token of his promise—instead of a ring. He said a ring would be too obvious. He said that the locket really meant a lot to him, so I had to believe he was serious. It was a long time before I figured out that it was just something his wife wouldn't miss."

"So you told Trey these were at Mrs. Swink's house?" Bobbie asked.

Darlene shook her head. "I didn't have to. He figured it out. He knew how much I used to hang out at her house back when we were kids. And he knew that since—you and I—well, that hers was the only safe place I had."

"Why didn't you come to me, Darlene?"

Darlene didn't say anything for a long time. "When it first happened, you were so mad at me. And he kept telling me that it would be the worst thing in the world if I told you. That you wouldn't believe me anyway. And you wouldn't have, would you?" She looked at Bobbie.

Bobbie couldn't deny that. She'd been among the first to embrace the new minister, and she'd been so proud when he'd appointed her head of the Kitchen Ministry. She'd been his staunchest supporter when one of the devils in the church had started that nasty little rumor about him. She remembered entrusting her child to him for counseling. Bobbie nodded her head in answer to Darlene's question.

"He said that you would stop me from seeing him, and then we couldn't get married. And I believed him. I was a fool. By the time I figured it out, it was too late. I had messed up too bad. You hated me. The only—"

"I didn't hate you, Darlene. You're my child. How could I hate you?"

"I hated myself, Mama. I hated the things I did. But sometimes it was all I could figure out to do." Darlene sighed. She took the envelope from Bobbie and put the locket and pictures back in it. She put the envelope in the Bible and snapped the strap back in the lock.

"Would you keep this for me, Mama, until Mrs. Swink comes back home?"

Bobbie took the Bible from her and put it in the bottom drawer of the dining room hutch. "Why don't we go to bed now, Darlene. It won't be long until morning."

Darlene shook her head. "No, I'll go."

"Baby, you don't have to leave. You're welcome to stay here."

Darlene shook her head again. "I don't want Monee to see me like this. Just give me a few bucks for cab fare."

"Sister Strickland. What a pleasure to see you." Reverend Jackson offered his hand, but Bobbie didn't take it. Instead, she sat down. She had thought about bringing Ray with her for this meeting, but decided it was something she needed to do alone. So he sat in the car and waited, while she sat here in the office.

His bookshelves were lined with theological treatises and tomes on psychology and counseling. On one shelf, nestled among the books, there was a photo of Jeralyn in a flowery ceramic frame. An ornate gold frame on the wall above his desk held a large portrait of Reverend Jackson in his black robe, accented with red velvet. One arm was crooked and a beautiful Bible was in his hand. His other hand rested on a brocade armchair. He was the very picture of piousness. Sitting behind his desk, he wore that same expression of patient piousness.

"What brings you around this way?" he asked with a smile.

Bobbie's eyes fell from the portrait and rested on his. "I'm here to speak with you about my daughter."

She could see the high alert in his eyes and knew at that moment that everything Darlene had told her last night was absolutely true.

"How is Darlene? She doesn't come to church, so I don't see her. I hope she's doing well." His hand moved to a figurine on his desk and began fingering it.

"She is now." There was no smile on Bobbie's face.

"Well, I'm glad to hear that."

"Marlon, I'm going to turn you in to the police."

He was so still, she thought he hadn't heard her. But his fingers ceased their rubbing on the figurine, so she knew that he had. She allowed the long silence to throb between them, her stare unblinking.

Finally he spoke. "Won't do you any good. The statute of

limitations is ten years. There's nothing they can charge me with now."

Slapping the taste out of his mouth wouldn't be enough for her. If she'd been a man, at that moment she would have hit him. She would have knocked the capped teeth out of his mouth so that he could never again give that toothy smile from the pulpit that she'd seen so many times. But she was a lady, so she didn't.

"But, Sister, I want you to know how sorry I am. The flesh is weak. But the Word calls on us to forgive and—"

"You low-down dog." The quiet words came through gritted teeth.

"There's no call for you to call me names. She was willing."

"She was sixteen. Just a child."

He rested his elbows on the desk and tented his hands against his mouth. "Well, we've all made mistakes and stumbled in our journey. We have to ask forgiveness and move on."

"But you see, we haven't been able to move on. My family has borne the pain of your weakness, and we've borne it alone. I think it's a burden that you should share with us."

"I have shared it. I gave her money. It was all just a mistake."

Bobbie stared at him. Her face was stone, her voice controlled. "Monee is a mistake?"

"I know you've been raising the child. If Darlene didn't give you the money, then it's not my fault."

"You can tell that to the congregation."

"Now, Sister Strickland," he said in a soothing tone, "our church is poised on the cusp of real success. We have a substantial building fund and are just about to break ground on the new building. You'll just cause confusion and problems. Don't allow yourself to be an instrument of Satan."

Bobbie raised one eyebrow. She'd been called some names in her life, but never an instrument of Satan.

"And think of Jeralyn. Think of what this would do to my poor wife. She's an innocent."

"Not as innocent as my child was."

When he saw the hardened look on her face, he knew it would take something more to convince her.

"Sister Strickland, you should give some thought to what people will say about you as a mother. To have allowed something like this to happen. You must not have provided the proper supervision for your child. Just think about the embarrassment such a revelation would cause to a woman in your position in the community. A principal. A woman charged with the care of many young lives. I think it's best for all of us to let sleeping dogs lie."

Bobbie thought of all the years she and Darlene had lost. All the years Monee and Darlene had lost. To him they were sleeping dogs. She stood up.

"You know, I was a member of Mount Moriah before you came. And I'll be a member after you're gone. I'll be in the choirstand in the morning. If you are there, fouling up the sanctuary, we'll see who will be the most embarrassed."

ᴗᴄ

The sun shone through the stained-glass windows. Bobbie smiled as she looked out over the congregation. In some ways it looked the same as when she'd joined Mt. Moriah as a student at Huston-Tillotson College. But it had changed. In nearly thirty years, she had seen a lot of the members grow up from children, and now they had children of their own. She had also seen a lot of them grow old and feeble.

The pastor's high-backed chair had been empty all through the service, and there had been frantic whispers among the associate ministers on the podium. Brother Harris's hastily prepared, extemporaneous sermon on the prodigal son, while not polished, had stirred more hearts than just hers. For the first time, Bobbie really noticed the new members he'd brought into the fold. Maybe in a way they were Brother Harris's prodigal sons. Maybe they had been away to places she didn't want to think about, but they had found a home now. Some of them dressed more casually than she approved of for church, but they were there most every Sunday. And from among them, an electric keyboard, two guitars, and drums had been added to the Music Ministry. A group of them had repaired and painted the old parsonage, which had been vacant for years. Now it was used for nightly AA and NA meetings—except Fridays, when the young adult singles held their weekly Bible study and social hour there. The church was growing and changing. New people had brought new talents and fresh ideas. Mt. Moriah would survive. She was sure of that.

When the children walked in, single file, from their service, she saw Monee go and sit next to Ray. Her heart was so full, she felt herself tearing up, but the organist's prelude signaled for the choir to sing the invitational hymn. Bobbie felt a strong sense of propriety about the church this morning. Not only did she belong to it, but it belonged to her. So she leaned over and whispered to the woman sitting in front

of her. Doretha turned and looked at her with a raised eyebrow, then gave a relinquishing shrug of her shoulders.
Bobbie walked to the microphone and pulled it from its
stand. The organ went quiet.

Bobbie closed her eyes and began. "Just As I Am." The
deacons lined the floor in front of the pulpit with their arms
extended, but no one came. When she started the second
verse, soft and intermittent clapping came from the congregation, and Bobbie opened her eyes. A young man she
hadn't seen in church for a long time was standing. He took
a hesitant step into the center aisle and began slowly walking toward the front. Instead of a suit and tie, he wore long,
baggy shorts, fancy sneakers, and an oversize T-shirt. With
each step his back became straighter, his gait more sure and
determined. The woman about her age who had been sitting next to him jumped up, threw her arms in the air, and
screamed. Bobbie felt that mother's joy all the way to her
heart, so she sang another verse while the woman walked to
the front shouting, "Thank you, Jesus! Thank you, Jesus!"
The woman opened her arms wide and wrapped them
around the young man, swaying him from side to side. Two
other women in the congregation shouted then, and a cho-
rus of "Amen" and "My Lord" emanated from all around
the sanctuary. Although it wasn't really necessary, the organist motioned for Bobbie to keep singing.

When she heard clapping again, Bobbie saw a young
woman walking up the side aisle. In a navy business suit, she
looked uncertain and scared. But only Bobbie would know
that. The others would only see her black eye and bruised
cheek and swollen lip. Bobbie's voice broke and she pressed
the mike to her lips to try to keep the tears in. As if they

had practiced it in rehearsal, the choir raised their voices to cover for her. From the back of the sanctuary, she heard Monee's voice:

"Mommie!"

Monee rushed to Darlene and put her arms around her waist. Darlene laid her head against Monee's and smoothed her hair.

Bobbie was filled with unspeakable joy. It took every ounce of strength she had to hold herself together. She took a deep breath, then another, then another. Holding the mike near her lips because she could only hum the melody, she stepped off the podium, waving her other hand in the air. Waving away the lost years. Waving away the pain. When she reached Darlene, she embraced her child.

Epilogue

BOBBIE PACED back and forth in the anteroom. She wished she'd worn her comfortable beige shoes, but the new satin pumps had been dyed to match the dress. She could hear the hushed organ music, in spite of the hum of the old window unit. Every now and then it shuddered in its battle with the dead heat of late August. She took a tissue from the box on the lamp table and patted her brow and temples, taking care not to ruin her makeup. An hour in the cosmetician's chair had almost killed her.

She looked at herself in the full-length mirror. The fitted bodice of the champagne chiffon dress was covered with iridescent sequins. The long sleeves were sheer, with six inches of pearl buttons at the wrist. The skirt flared around her calves. It wasn't white, but it was beautiful and she felt beautiful wearing it.

"Why don't you sit down, Barbara. Save your feet. They'll tell us when it's time," her father said.

"Okay. I guess I should, huh? I'm just so nervous." She sat on the couch next to his wheelchair.

"What's to be nervous about? The man bought you a house. You think he's gonna run off now?" He smiled at his only daughter.

"You don't think it's silly, me having this big wedding—at my age?"

"I think you deserve it. And I do too."

Bobbie pressed her lips together and smiled back at him.

"Bobbie, I like this fellow. I feel like I'm leaving you in good hands. I can go peacefully now." He pulled a handkerchief from his breast pocket and quickly dabbed at one eye.

"You just stop that kind of talk right now. You're not going anywhere. Darby needs you to help him get his practice established down there in Houston."

"Yeah, I guess you're right. I'd better hang on a couple of more years."

The sanctuary was full of well-wishers from the congregation and teachers from Bobbie's school. Even Bill Gibson had had the nerve to come. Or maybe he just didn't have the nerve not to come. Dr. Darby Strickland, DDS, served as usher, escorting Bobbie's close friends to sit in the reserved section. When it was time for the ceremony to begin, he allowed Mrs. Swink to take his arm. Mr. Rafaeli followed them up front to the bride's side of the aisle. Darby sat Mrs. Swink in the traditional place for the bride's mother. Vivian Kline, her husband, and their two little girls were just behind them. In the same row, Mrs. Downs and Idalia sat next to Jimbo in his mismatched suit.

At precisely seven o'clock, the new minister took his place in front. He was a little nervous because this was his first wedding at Mt. Moriah and it was different from any he'd done. Glancing at the bride's side, he couldn't quite figure the family out, but he'd learned that family is those who take care of you, and whom you take care of. And sometimes blood doesn't have anything to do with it.

He'd only been here at Mt. Moriah for a month, and he hadn't been able to get the straight story on what had happened to the former pastor. What he'd heard from a few of the gossips was unbelievable, and he knew that they would bear watching. What he did know was that it was a growing church with a substantial building fund and a cohesive Deacons Board—and he was grateful to God for the opportunity that seemed to have just fallen in his lap.

At the minister's nod, Ray and his mother walked in from a side door. Sister Caldwell looked delighted in her unusual role as best man. Monee walked down the center aisle, dropping silver petals from her basket, which matched her pewter-colored dress. Darlene was right behind her, in a more grown-up version of the dress, carrying a bouquet of ivory roses.

The music changed to the wedding march.

"That sounds like our call, baby. It's show time. Let's go."

Bobbie squatted down so that her eyes were even with her dad's. "I wish Mama could be here too."

"Baby, we've waited a long time for this day. Virgie's watching. You can be sure about that. I'm just glad I can be here for it. Now, wipe your eyes."

Standing in the vestibule, Bobbie held her bouquet of ivory roses in her right hand and held her daddy's hand that the stroke had left limp with her other. The ushers opened the double doors to the sanctuary, and together they started down the aisle. Mr. Strickland maneuvered the motorized wheelchair at Bobbie's pace.

Ray's army buddies had stationed themselves on the aisle seats, and each gave a crisp military salute as the bride passed them.

"Who gives this woman away?" the minister asked.

"I do," Mr. Strickland said from his chair. Then he moved it to the side of the aisle, next to Mrs. Swink. Ray joined Bobbie, offering his arm. Bobbie shifted her bouquet to her other hand and slipped her arm through the crook of his.

The minister performed the traditional wedding ceremony, with a few changes the couple had made. Then he pronounced them "husband and wife," as they had requested. "You may salute your bride."

With a big grin on his face, Ray looked into Bobbie's eyes. In a low voice he asked, "Are you crazy about me yet, woman?"

Bobbie pressed her lips together in a crooked smile. She whispered back, "Only me and that old owl know."

Dear Reader Friend,

These continue to be exciting times for us. So many books, so little time.

I always write of "marvelously mature" heroines. The inspiration for *Everything in Its Place* came from an article in a July 1999 edition of *The Villager,* an African-American newspaper in Austin. I was struck by the story of a thirty-eight-year-old woman who had assumed the care of two infant grandchildren and raised them to adulthood. Then I looked around and saw that many women of all races and from all walks of life were raising grandchildren. The common denominator was that they never got a break from child-rearing responsibilities that they surely had expected. But, I'd bet, they still have a need for romance in their lives, so I've tried to give them a little.

I met so many of you through the survey in *Dangerous Dilemmas,* and it was so much fun that I included one in this book too. If you have a few minutes, I'd love to hear from you.

Evelyn

1. In *Dangerous Dilemmas,* I intentionally did not describe the physical attributes of the characters. In this book, I didn't realize that I hadn't done it until I finished. Could you "see" Bobbie and Ray?
2. What did they look like to you (coloring, height, weight, etc.)?
3. Are you, or is someone close to you, raising a grand-child?

4. If so, can you share the reason why?
5. Do you view the incidence of grandparents raising grandchildren as a new phenomenon, a repeat of a pattern in the 1930s and 40s, or no change?

Respond to:
    PO Box 142495
    Austin, TX 78714
    or evelyn@evelynpalfrey.com

There is a wealth of information about grandparenting at www.aarp.org/grandparents/.